Shadows by the Lighthouse

A Novel

by
Melissa Puritis

This is a work of fiction. Names, characters, places, and incidents either are the product of the author's imagination or are used fictitiously. Any resemblance to actual persons, living or dead, events, or locales is entirely coincidental.

Copyright © 2022 by Melissa Puritis

All rights reserved. No part of this book may be reproduced or used in any manner without written permission of the copyright owner except for the use of quotations in a book review.

First paperback edition 2022

Cover art by Gabe Lovejoy

ISBN 978-0-578-34503-1

For more information please contact www.melissapuritis.weebly.com

For Avery,
my partner in crime and little adventurer.
May you always dream big and love fiercely.
This is for you, bear.

Chapter 1

Ten boxes and a few trash bags: this is what Avery Fowler's thirteen years has amounted to. It's all been shoved onto a moving truck, and Avery now leans against his mom's Jeep and stares at a house that is technically no longer his. How can you miss something that is standing right in front of you? Avery's not sure, but he does.

He feels his mother come alongside him. She wraps an arm around him and kisses the top of his head, the mess of his dirty blond hair; he didn't bother to brush it this morning.

"Our family had a lot of great memories here," she says, smiling despite the tears coming to her eyes. Her dark hair is piled on her head in a messy bun, and Avery notices the dark circles under her eyes that aren't usually there.

"Do you mean the two of us?" asks Avery, his voice filled with anger. And he has a lot of anger because he doesn't want to move, and he especially doesn't want to move because of his dad, the member of his family that has always been too busy to actually be part of their family.

"That's not fair, Avery," says his mom. "Your dad works hard, and he loves us. This will be an adventure for all of us to face together. And hopefully, you will find new things to do and be passionate about, instead of just video games."

Avery gives his mother the side eye. He doesn't want to move. Life has been going really well for him at Sounding Springs Middle School. He's on the soccer team, and even though he wasn't the star, he didn't just ride the bench, which is good enough for him. He had his lunch table full of friends, and he hoped to finally talk to Becca Green this school year. Now all of that's being taken from him because his dad has a new job ten hours away. Sure, his parents claim there are benefits to the move, but that doesn't matter to him. It just isn't fair. Period.

"I'm on the soccer team!" he reminds her.

"Yeah, but maybe you'll have a coach that inspires you to do more, to be more and really push yourself," she says. "Look at this as a time to really find out just how incredible you are, kid. Give it a chance. Your dad is ready to go, so hop in his truck. I will see you in a few hours."

She hugs him tightly and waves over to his dad, the creator of this mess. Avery stomps over and climbs into his father's Chevy truck to make his way to Summerset Island, North Carolina. Staring out the window of the passenger's side, he silently says goodbye to the house he spent the past thirteen years in, to the park where his mom taught him how to play catch, to his best friend Matt's house. Everything seemed to go by in a blur, and Avery hopes he doesn't forget how things look. He hopes even more that people don't forget about him.

His father's voice slices through his thoughts. "Thanks for

agreeing to keep me company on the ride. Plus, I would like to think I have better taste in music than your mother. I mean, how long can a person listen to Taylor Swift?" If his mother had a choice, the answer would be forever with some Harry Styles mixed in, but Avery didn't say anything. "Moving isn't the end of the world, Avery. I know it feels like it is right now, but I promise, you will see that there are plenty of benefits to change."

"Oh yeah, like what?" Avery turns his head to face his dad; there was nothing to see anyway since their neighborhood was now behind them. His arms are crossed, but he realizes that, that seems childish, like a temper tantrum, so he rests an arm on the door instead.

His father is a patient, kind man. He has a laugh that fills a room and has never met a stranger. Avery's friends have always been surprised by how cool his dad is; they assume he won't be laid back because of his job and because he looks a little rough around the edges, as his mother would say. His dad is smiling now, his eyes on the road, and says, "Well for starters, we will be living on the beach. Literally, the expanse of the ocean will be right outside our back door. Your mother is going to hate how much sand you'll track inside the house. The soccer team at your new school is a good one. Not undefeated, but strong. The coach says there is a lot of potential this year, and he is excited to meet-"

"You talked to the soccer coach?" Avery interrupts.

"Of course. I wanted to make sure there would be room for you on the team, and if not, I wanted to find a backup plan before we arrived. There are multiple travel teams in the area, so if you didn't play for the school, we have options. There are two officers at the station that have sons who will be in your grade, and they have agreed to meet you and show you around tomorrow. And, what I hope really sells it, is that even though this will be a promotion of sorts, I will be home more. I should make it home for dinner almost every night, and I should be able to see almost all of your games. We'll feel more like a family."

And even Avery had to admit that's important. In New Jersey, his dad was captain of vice, the illegal drug unit for their city's police department. His hours were never consistent, and when his cell phone for work rang, which it did a lot, he had to go. It didn't matter if it was in the middle of Christmas dinner or cutting birthday cake, Avery's dad took his job very seriously and always answered, always went in. That left Avery with Mrs. Fowler most of the time, and yeah, his mom is awesome, but sometimes, you really want your dad there. Now he would be chief of police in Summerset Island. The promotion to chief should make there be more work, not less, but the town is small, the crime rate almost nonexistent. It's a tourist community, bustling in the summers and quiet in the winters.

His dad, now Chief Fowler, continues, "Your mom and I know this is hard for you. We understand that you are giving up a lot. I do think, though, big picture, this move is the best thing for all of us. Can you trust me?"

Avery thinks before responding. His dad had never steered

him wrong, at least not when he's been around. But how often has that really been? His mom would want him to try, though, and since no one is going to give him what he wants anyway, it doesn't make sense to say no. So he says yes, and then they agree on a radio station.

"Alright, so tell me about this Becca Green," says his dad.

Avery groans, his brain cringing at the thought of having this conversation.

"No, Dad. Just, no." He turns up the radio and keeps his eyes straight ahead on the road, across a few state lines to their new life in Summerset Island and away from the comfort that his old life held.

Chapter 2

He wakes to his mother poking him on the head, his mound of pillows and blankets all scattered around him. They decided to camp out in the living room for their first night in their new house. His mother dug through boxes and pulled out every pillow, comforter, throw blanket, and sleeping bag she could find. Avery has to admit that the house is everything his dad promised. His mom keeps talking about the open floor plan and the beams and other rustic details, but Avery likes how they can see the ocean from anywhere in their living and kitchen area. Last night, when they were settling in, the kitchen was flooded with pink and orange from the sunset. They opened the windows so they could hear the waves hitting the shore, ordered pizza from a local restaurant, ate off paper plates and drank water out of coffee cups. They sat and told stories and then watched a movie on the laptop. It was disorganized, and the floor wasn't all that comfortable, but it was still nice to all be together, like a family, finally the three of them.

He swats at his mom's hand, but she persists. That is something to note about his mother; she's a teacher, so nothing he does shocks or intimidates her, and he's tried. She takes it all in strides, smiles as she goes, and survives thanks to iced coffee and sarcasm. And hugs; she is a big hugger. Her brown hair frames her face as she bends over Avery to tap again. "Your dad is about to leave for the station, kiddo."

"Okay, good for him," Avery mumbles, trying to pull the covers back over his head. He doesn't want to wake up; it probably means doing work.

"Oh, so you didn't want to meet Landon and Owen and start this business of making new friends? My bad, I thought life is so terrible without kids your age to be friends with, and it's the end of the world because you wouldn't know anyone, but I'll tell your dad to go on without you." She begins walking away.

"I'm up, I'm up, no need to tell Dad anything," Avery says, wiping the sleep from his eyes and heading to the bathroom. Five minutes later he walks back past his mother who kisses the top of his head while wrapping her arms around him and handing him a strawberry Pop Tart, calling after him to have fun.

He climbs into his dad's truck, trying to ignore the butterflies that are soaring around in his stomach. His dad seems to be in no hurry, taking a sip of his coffee before backing out of the driveway. They drive toward the police station, and Chief Fowler points out where Avery's new school is, where the ice cream shop is, and nods towards the one and only Starbucks in town. Avery turns to his father with his mouth open in shock, and his father raises his hands in a mock surrender. "I know, dude, I don't know how they survive either. Maybe it's a southern thing."

The police station is much smaller than the one his father

worked at before. It could almost pass for a small house, white siding and black shutters, nestled in by the pier where the ferry brings in herds of tourists. In the distance, he can see the lighthouse with its pirate museum.

Avery hops out of the truck and stares up at the lighthouse. "It looks really old," he pronounces, shading his eyes from the sun while trying to see what the top of the lighthouse looks like.

"Yeah, it should," his dad says. "It's one of the oldest on the East coast. It aided pirates and Civil War soldiers, too. It's seen a lot."

"Pirates, huh? It's too bad they don't still exist. That would make things interesting," Avery says, now giving his attention to the museum in a small building, acting as gatekeeper to the lighthouse.

"Well, son, in a lot of ways they do," his dad says. "It's why the Coast Guard patrols the oceans as much as they do. And there are other ways to be a pirate these days. You just need to broaden your definition."

Avery considers this and wonders how his father knows so much about so much; hopefully someday he would have that much information just stored away for the right moment. He follows his dad into the police station, trying not to act excited about seeing where his dad will be working and, of course, meeting the two boys because that would make him lame.

The station is small, with a secretary's desk placed only a few short feet away from the front door. It seems to be mostly one large office with desks organized against the walls, providing each officer a workspace. Avery knows there are only a handful of people who work in the station, and he wonders which door leads to his dad's new office. A smiling woman greets them with a whole lot of pep.

"Hey, Chief Fowler. We're so excited you're here. And you must be Avery; wow, you look just like your dad, but I'm sure you hear that all the time."

He does, but he doesn't mind it, so Avery gives this woman a smile. She is tiny, barely taller than he is, with blond hair pulled into a tight bun at the top of her head. As friendly as she is and as quickly as she greeted them, Avery assumed she's the receptionist, but now that he is looking, she is wearing the black police uniform, badge and all, her name tag reading Brown.

She continues speaking, though she has turned toward a desk Avery assumes to be hers over against the far wall. "I have something for you. Technically it's for your whole family, but Avery, I picked it out for you." She extends her hand to him, and Avery sees she has tickets, three of them. "There's a local professional soccer team in the neighboring town. It might not be the World Cup, but they play hard."

Avery didn't even need his father to remind him to say thank you. This is a gift he actually wants, and he thanks Officer Brown multiple times, causing her to laugh. "Well, a little birdie told me that you're a huge soccer fan. In fact, if your parents don't want to go, maybe you can take the two knuckleheads in the conference room that are eating all my donuts even though they've been told repeatedly they are for officers only." She says this last part with her voice raised in warning.

A "We're not eating all of them!" comes from the next room followed by a "Busted!", and the chief waves Avery over to make introductions. Two boys are sprawled in the overstuffed chairs, donuts in hands, chocolate in the corners of their mouths. One has unruly curly brown hair, and the other's hair is buzzed close, blonde like the sun tried to steal all of its color. Both look like they have spent a good deal of time at the beach, made even more obvious by their board shorts. They wear looks of guilt from their donut pillaging.

But that's not Avery's dad's style. From experience, Avery knows he doesn't sweat the small stuff, so Chief Fowler just says, "As long as you always leave a chocolate one for me, we're good. Hide it in my office if necessary." He smiles widely and shakes both of their hands before introducing Avery. The curly headed one is Landon, and now that they are standing, it is obvious how tall Owen is.

It's Owen that says, "Hey man, grab a donut and let's head to the beach." So Avery does, and they do, saying goodbye to Avery's dad and Officer Brown and walking down the street towards the shoreline. They walk side by side, with no real hurry to them.

"Do you surf?" Landon asks Avery.

"Oh man, these donuts are ridonkulous! I see why you steal them from the station." He's licking his fingers to get every last bit of goodness. "No, I have never surfed before, but I'm down to learn if you guys could show me a few things."

"Yeah, Officer Brown only brings the best," says Landon. "She's cool, and she has these two massive dogs; you'll see them all running around on the beach together. And we can definitely teach you how to surf. It's pretty much a requirement to live here."

The boys walk down the beach, and Avery takes note of the groups of families all camped in the sand, the bright colors from towels and umbrellas, the pounding of the waves, the squawking of birds and small children. Owen explains that it is always this crowded during tourist season, so they rarely bring much with them to the sand so that they didn't have to worry about finding a place to leave it. Avery observes the huge houses sprawling on the other side of the dunes in neutral shades; he had expected bright colors, like what they had in New Jersey, and said as much, but Landon explained that the people with money on the island preferred to show it tastefully with obscenely large houses instead of color. The three boys laugh and then share about the things they have in common, the video games they play, the type of music they listen to, movies they like, and of course soccer.

"I'm hoping to be team captain this year," says Owen. "Finally! The coach only lets eighth graders be captain, so even though last year's captain was a joke, he got the job because he was older. Seniority or whatever. But not anymore. The field's ours!"

Avery smiles at the thought, trying to hide his nerves. He wonders how strong of a player Owen actually is, and if Avery himself is actually good enough to even make the team. His dad said he called the coach, but no one here has seen him play. Even his dad can't vouch for his ability; his dad's never been to one of Avery's games.

"Earth to Avery! Wow, you just zoned right out! Is that a Jersey thing?" Owen says.

"It's just my brain adjusting to how slow you Southerners talk!" They laugh.

"We were asking about your dad. He seems pretty cool, bro. Those tattoos, and he is so much younger than the last chief. She would have been pissed about the donuts. But your dad seems pretty chill, like you could hang out with him," says Owen.

Avery has limited experience having fun with his dad, but he's not ready to admit this to Landon and Owen; they are still essentially randos. "He is, and my mom is pretty cool too. You can meet her if you want; she's right up there on the porch, and we could grab something to drink," Avery says as he points up to his house. He's impressed that he recognized it so easily, though it's probably more so that he recognized his mom's bright pink hat, but the island is pretty clearly divided: a section for big houses and a section for small ones. The house is what his mother refers to as cozy; she explained that it's a bungalow, as if Avery cares to keep track of types of houses.

The three boys climb the steps up to the house, and Avery's mom stops whatever she was doing, her eyes grow wide and bright as a smile spreads across her face.

"Hey, guys, I'm Emily." She sticks her hand out and shakes the two boys' hands. Owen and Landon exchange looks, and Avery can tell from their barely concealed smiles that she has won them over. Emily Fowler is just a cool mom. Sandwiches are offered as compensation for manual labor; the boys move the porch furniture around at least three times until Avery's mom finally likes the placement. Now sitting around the table and eating the sandwiches, Avery mentions the tickets Officer Brown gave him.

"So, Mom, Officer Brown gave me tickets to this soccer game, and she said they were for our family, but I was thinking that maybe, if you and Dad weren't into it, I could bring these guys."

"Sure, I don't see why not. You boys just check with your parents, and either your dad or I can drop you all off." The boys exchange high fives before devouring what remains of their sandwiches.

Landon and Owen help Avery put his bed together so that he wouldn't have to sleep on the floor again tonight, arguing over the directions, over the right name of the tools, and laughing at each other like they have been friends for years and not hours.

It makes Avery think of Matt. Landon and Owen are clearly tight, so will there really be room for him? Are they legit into being his friend, or are their dads making them? But, putting furniture together is really going beyond just showing him around, so maybe he should relax and just hope for the best. If nothing else, at least he won't be sleeping on the floor.

***

Bed assembled, they go back out into the sunshine so the boys could give Avery a proper tour of the town.

The road is narrow but quiet, and Landon and Owen walk right in the center of it.

"So, you guys aren't worried about traffic?" says Avery, thinking about what would happen if he did this back home.

Owen looks both ways, up and down the road, "What traffic? Most people don't drive anything but their golf cart. The island's so tinesy, cars aren't needed unless you are headed off island."

Landon walks a little ahead and calls, "You're lucky, Avery, your parents are pretty chill. Why did you guys come down here? I mean, I bet your dad was into all kinds of intense stuff up in Jersey."

Avery shrugs. "I guess. He was crazy busy all the time, though. That's why we're here. So he can slow down or whatever."

"Well, he will slow way down here. It's pretty boring. I can't think of the last interesting thing my dad told us about."

Owen scoffs a little. "Maybe about little old ladies and their cats, or tourists who accidently attempt to break into a home because they forget which massive beach house they have rented for the week. Down here, there are no high-speed chases, no crazy armed robberies, no assassination attempts."

"Who would be assassinated down here?" Avery laughs. "Or in Jersey for that matter? That seems a little extra." Who are these kids, and what movies are they watching, Avery thinks.

"You know what I mean," Owen says, shoving Avery. "I wish

sometimes that a little more happened here. I want to be a cop like my dad, but I need a little more adventure. Something to flex about other than rescuing kittens!"

Avery knows his father has seen plenty of adventures, but he certainly hasn't. These guys are talking like his father lets him tag along, but the truth is, he barely even knows his dad's stories. I bet their dads tell them everything about their days; funny, they have no idea how good they have it, Avery thinks.

Landon, still up in front, points to the park ahead. "They are having their weekly market. It's not like a farmer's market, so no worries, it's not lame. It's more like a flea market or a yard sale. You can find really cool stuff."

The boys walk towards the market, Avery asking more questions about what school would be like and when they would have to start. "In Jersey, we don't go back to school until September. What kind of classes are you guys in, like honors or anything? Are there a lot of kids in each class?"

"I'm on the AIG track, but Owen and I still have most of our classes together. Classes are kind of big. Even though the number of locals on the island is pretty small, the other beaches go to the same school," says Landon.

Avery relaxes; maybe they will end up in the same classes then. How bad would it suck to make these new friends but still end up alone on the first day?

"Maybe this will help you," Owen says, holding out an old school Magic 8-Ball toy. Avery worries he may have asked too many questions or that Owen's irritated about the assassination comment, so he reaches out for the toy without saying anything.

Stacks of comic books draw Owen and Landon's attention, but Avery just looks at the toy in his hand. He hears someone walk up behind him and turns to see a man about his dad's age wearing a t-shirt with the Wu-Tang logo, ripped jeans, and flip flops. Flip flops... He is going to need to get more, or he has no chance of fitting in.

"Are you a local or just visiting?" the man asks, resting a hand on the table and glancing at the toy in Avery's hand. Avery assumes this must be his table.

"Cool shirt. I'm a local, I guess. My family just moved here."

"A boy your age knowing about the Wu? That's impressive. It's nice to know people are raising children well. If you moved here recently, I guess you are Chief Fowler's kid. Am I right?" the man smiles, and Avery has to remind himself that in a small town, it is not suspicious for a stranger to know this about him. He feels even more comfortable when Landon and Owen acknowledge the man, so he nods and smiles as a response. The man reaches out his hand to shake Avery's free one and introduces himself as Andrew, the owner of the music shop.

"Oh, no wonder you have the cool shirt, then," Avery says with a laugh before asking what kind of music shop it is.

"I sell a little bit of everything," Andrew says. "If I don't have an instrument, I can get it. I also have records and sound systems of all kinds. I'm trying to keep those alive, you know? More than just online radio and what not. And I give guitar lessons. Do you play?

"No, I have a drum kit at home," Avery says. "Or at least, I will once we unpack. I wouldn't mind learning how to play the guitar, too, though."

Owen comes over to ask Andrew a question about a specific Spiderman edition, and in the quiet moment, Avery looks back at the forgotten Magic 8-Ball in his hand. "Will I find fun and adventure here?" he asks the plastic toy.

It is certain. Avery smiles and decides to buy it. He has no idea what is in store for him in this new town, but he hopes the Magic 8-Ball is right.

Chapter 3

Avery wakes up to the quiet and stares at the ceiling of his new room. The walls are still bare, the shelves mostly empty; he's been trying to ignore it, but he misses his home. Keeping busy has helped him pretend otherwise. For the past few days, he has spent hours in the water trying to learn to surf, and right now his body is feeling it from the constant paddling and the constant falling. He hit his face on the board more than once, though he didn't want to admit it to Owen and Landon and look like a fool.

Despite being sore, he gets up. Today is going to be a big day. His father is being sworn in as police chief in some sort of fancy ceremony. At least, he assumes it is going to be a fancy ceremony, though here in North Carolina things seem to be much different than in New Jersey. The pace is slower, and people are always saying hello and asking about your family. It seemed like everywhere he went with Landon and Owen yesterday, someone was telling them to tell their mothers this and this or ask their fathers that and that. It's so different from New Jersey, the lack of anonymity, and thanks to his dad, people are already recognizing Avery, too. It's a little unnerving, but Avery tries not to be creeped out because, really, it seems kind of cool, this sense of belonging. This feeling that people know you and care about your life.

He stretches out one last time in his bed before reaching for the Magic 8-Ball. "Is today the day I stand up on my surfboard?" he asks the tiny oracle.

As I see it, yes.

With this affirmation, Avery rushes to find his board shorts and heads to the beach. He doesn't even feel the need to wait on Owen and Landon; he hopes they will be along eventually, and there are plenty of other surfers in the water each morning. Plus, his parents are sitting on the back porch keeping an eye on him. His parents... his dad hasn't left for work yet, and if Avery can pull this off, his dad will see his accomplishment and not just hear about it later. No pressure or anything, but he wants this. Maybe one day he can even teach his dad to surf, too; they could do it together.

Avery waits for the right wave. That's one thing Owen stressed to be important during their first lesson: not every wave is for you, so you can't get discouraged when they don't work out like you think they will. He sees other surfers picking up waves that he has let go by, but he reasons this is just giving him time to get comfortable, to get into the right headspace. Eventually he sees a swell that seems to have his name on it, one that won't pass him by or collapse before he even gets to it. He paddles his arms as fast as he can, shoving his hands into the water again and again until he feels the wave solid underneath him. With quick, deft motions, he pushes himself up to standing, keeping his legs bent as his friends taught him to and stretching his arms out in attempts to keep his balance. He's sure it doesn't look cool or graceful, but he is up. He's surfing, and it seems like the real beginning for his new life here at the beach.

Avery can see his parents cheering for him on the porch. Other kids might be embarrassed, but Avery knows he's lucky, and that if they hadn't moved here, his dad wouldn't be around to see this moment. Well, really the moment wouldn't exist for a lot of reasons. He paddled out again, hoping for another wave to try to get more practice, but he realizes he isn't good at reading the waves just yet. Practice.

Time goes past, but he doesn't get another wave. Avery lets out a huge huff of frustration, but before he can talk himself into giving up, Officer Brown is out in the water beside him on her board.

"I didn't know you surfed," he says.

She laughs. "There's probably quite a bit you don't know about me, Avery." She splashes him and asks him how it is going. They bob up and down on their boards, and he admits that he isn't sure when to try to catch a wave. She nods and explains to him that what might help him for now is to move a little closer to shore, just until he gets more comfortable popping up and timing things right. "It's a lot easier to rise in on whitewash and get the feel of the water. It'll help you build confidence, too."

She paddles toward the shoreline with him, helping him find a good spot to sit and wait. And when he catches the next wave in, she cheers loudly, clapping and whooping. After trying a few more, they both walk up to the beach.

"Good job, Avery. It's not an easy thing, and you are catching on quickly. Keep trying. I'll see you this afternoon, okay?"

They say goodbye, and she gives a quick wave to his parents on the porch while he walks to the house, covered in sand and salt, loving it.

***

Later that day, Avery straightens his tie and stands with his mother in the Town Hall garden. He sees Owen and Landon beside their fathers, and it dawns on him that they never made it out to the beach this morning. He was so excited to have stood up and have his dad see it, and then have Officer Brown out there with him, he somehow forgot that they bailed on him. Or did they? Were clear plans ever made, or did Avery just assume they were coming because they had the past few days? Maybe that was it, and maybe he's over thinking it. They don't have to hang out all the time, he guesses.

Officer Brown is off to the side, giving him a little wave, her two dogs seated next to her panting quietly. They, along with a few other people from town and other officers Avery has yet to meet, watch as Avery's dad officially becomes Chief Fowler of Summerset Island. His dad's eyes are clear, his mouth in a straight line as he listens to the obligations he is to fulfill, the challenge to keep this place safe. His mom's face has a huge proud smile, her eyes gleaming and glued to his dad. Avery wonders if she's happy to be here, after leaving her old classroom and all her friends, even ones from when she was in high school. She loves his dad and their family, and she always supports them both, so maybe she is.

When the mayor is finished and Chief Fowler's badge is fastened to his shirt, his pins placed on his lapel, Avery and his friends all shout and cheer.

Everyone is invited back to Avery's house. Mrs. Fowler and some of the officers prepared sandwiches and salads, kabobs and quiches, enough food for the whole town. Avery and his friends load their plates and escape to the backyard. They play with Officer Brown's dogs, two huge chocolate labradoodles whose fur make them look like teddy bears. Thor stands next to Owen now, almost half his height, but despite the intimidating size, the dogs seem happy to lick every face they come across. The boys take turns throwing balls for them and they all run around in the surf. When the sun drops from the sky, they listen to Officer Brown talk about astronomy, how to find the North Star and why they might need it someday, how it could help them navigate.

"Yeah, but why couldn't we just use our phones, Officer Brown?" Landon asks.

"You never know where life will take you and why. It doesn't hurt to be prepared for a bit of the unexpected," she says.

More people came out to the beach, eventually leading to a big game of soccer, kids against adults. Someone mentions how late it is, and families begin leaving, one by one at first, and then more. Officer Brown, now in uniform because her shift began in the midst of the celebration, stays to help them clean up, and so did Landon and Owen's families. Avery doesn't remember anything after closing his eyes, that's how tired he is.

And when he wakes up, everything is different.

Chapter 4

Waves are crashing just outside the window. Avery's excited to get back on his board, but first, he needs food. His stomach growls with aggression that will not be ignored. He finds some dry board shorts and makes his way to the kitchen, hoping that he will find something better than a Pop-Tart to eat. Somehow, he's hungry despite all that he ate last night.

His mother is in the kitchen, mouth in a tight line, eyes staring in the distance. He's seen that look on his mother's face before, many times if he's being honest, when his dad is at work, on days when his task is a little more dangerous than others. But this isn't Jersey; this is a sleepy little beach town. His dad has to be fine, doesn't he?

"Mom? What's wrong?" he asks. "Where's Dad?"

"Dad's at work, honey." She doesn't smile, her lips turn down instead, and her eyes are a little red. "There was an accident last night. Officer Brown was shot while on duty. Your father is there trying to find out what happened, but unfortunately, by the time anyone responded, it was too late. Officer Brown didn't make it."

Officer Brown, the tiny woman with the huge dogs, the woman who seemed to have a smile for everyone, who was kind to Avery before she even met him, getting him the tickets to the soccer game, is gone. How could that be right? His mom wrapped her arms around him and told him she is sorry, though he isn't sure what she possibly had to be sorry for. Maybe for the fact that their fresh start has now fallen apart.

"Do you want to talk about it?" she asks.

He doesn't, though. This isn't like two years ago when his grandfather passed away from a long illness. There was a reason for that. There was scientific information and the knowledge that his grandfather had lived a long and happy life. Officer Brown was young, though, probably a little younger than his parents. Good people, good officers, are not supposed to get hurt. This didn't make sense, and Avery knows his mom doesn't have the answers that he needs. She squeezes him tightly and offers him breakfast, but he is no longer hungry. He goes back to his room to call his friends and see what they know, what they're doing. While he waits for their response, he asks the Magic 8-Ball the only question he can think of: "What happened to Officer Brown?"

Better not tell you now.

Well, what does that mean, he wonders.

***

He meets up with Owen and Landon at a coffee shop close to the ferry slip, tucked into a booth in the back. All three boys wear rumpled clothes, barely matching, hair all askew; none of them wear a smile. Not even the beach can cheer them up today. Their smoothies sit mostly full, and their eyes go everywhere but each other. "This is crazy," Owen says. "I can't believe she's gone. How's your dad, Landon?"

Landon's dad had been the first one to the scene. Landon shrugs. "I haven't actually seen him, but I know he's upset. He really likes her. I mean, everyone does. And I don't think he has ever witnessed anything like that. Stuff like this doesn't happen in Summerset Island."

Avery knows his friends feel the same way he does: useless, unable to do anything helpful. They are kids, and kids just get pushed to the side when stuff like this happens. He remembers overhearing so many of his parents' conversations, things that they didn't think he was old enough to hear. And sure, maybe sometimes they are right, but at the end of the day, this is life, and Officer Jones is part of his life. Or she should be. He sits up straighter, an idea forming in his mind. "Maybe we should go to her house. We could hang out with the dogs, take care of them."

Owen sits up taller too, "Yeah, she would really appreciate that. Let's do it."

The boys pick up their cups and make their way down the few blocks to Officer Brown's house. Avery's surprised to be met by police officers; his dad is not there, but Owen's is. Owen's dad, Sergeant Martinez, waves them over; he's tired, Avery can tell by dark circles under his eyes and lines around his mouth where a smile should be. His black uniform stands out against the brightness of the sunshine.

"What are you boys doing here?" He crosses his arms, and his voice is stern and a little irritated. "We're in the middle of an investigation. I know you all really liked Brown, which is why you need to give us some room to do our jobs."

"We know, Dad, but we thought maybe we could take Thor and Hulk for a while," Owen says. "They must be so confused, and maybe they are getting in the way."

His dad nods his head and explains that the dogs are with a neighbor. He points out the house. Landon takes off in that direction, Avery and Owen right after him. The neighbors are an older couple, and they are quick to explain that while they are happy to help, they are also happy not to have to walk such huge dogs.

"I know your fathers are going to clear this all up quickly," the older man says. "It's just such a tragedy."

The woman shakes her head. "I just don't understand it," she says. "She was the nicest woman. She always came over to help in the garden, or she brought the dogs over to say hello with some cookies or brownies she had recently made. She was the best neighbor." Fresh tears stream down her face, and Avery has no idea what to say because he does not know this woman, and he realizes more and more that he didn't know Officer Brown like these other people did. Does he have the right to be so upset?

The boys accept the leashes and lead the dogs away. They decide to let the two play at the beach, and later they will figure out whose house the dogs would stay at, at least for tonight. Maybe they could take turns, because how can their parents say no considering the circumstances?

***

Hours pass, and eventually Avery hears the sound of a car door slamming nearby, probably his dad's. The crew heads toward the house in order to find out what happened to their friend. When the boys walk into the house, they find Avery's parents with their arms around each other, both obviously upset and in mid-conversation. Chief Fowler notices them first, and he says hello and tells them to come in.

"I know you boys have a lot of questions and that you have a vested interest in what happened to Officer Brown. I have a lot of questions, too." As he speaks, they move to the kitchen counter, the three boys taking seats on the bright blue metal stools at the counter while Mrs. Fowler opens and closes cabinets. Avery finally realizes she is looking for bowls and getting water for the dogs, and he tells himself he needs to do better if he is going to be responsible for them.

"This is what we know for sure. Officer Brown was patrolling around the base of the lighthouse; everything had been routine throughout the night. Around 2:55 this morning she radioed into dispatch, letting them know she was 'out with three' and to stand by. A few minutes later, the dispatcher could hear Brown say, 'There's no reason for anyone to have a gun on this island.'" Chief Fowler pauses here for a moment and just stares into space.

Avery is upset about Officer Brown, but he is also upset for his father. Because he is chief, Avery's dad will hold himself responsible; she was his officer. He has only officially been chief for a day, so how could this be his fault?

Avery's mom hands his dad a glass of water. After taking a swallow, the chief continues his story: "The dispatcher said that there was a pause or a shuffle and then she heard Officer Brown's voice again, this time asking the perpetrator to lower the weapon, and again to put the gun down please. The dispatcher said that she could hear the fear in Brown's voice. Then there's this high-pitched squeal before the radio goes dead. Other officers, having heard the requests and the squeal over their radios, tried to reach her over the radio and then by cell phone, but there was no response. Landon, your father made it to the lighthouse first. She was deceased by the time he made it there."

He's holding back, Avery thinks. There's more to the story. Chief Fowler maybe wants to end it there, but more could be told and more would be told by the news crews, so there is really no point to hide it; even thirteen-year-olds can watch the news.

"She was their friend," Avery's mom says softly while she scratches his back.

The room is silent in waiting, even the dogs lay down, paws crossed. He lets out a loud whoosh of air before speaking again. "He found her body by her truck. It seems that she was shot with her own weapon. Landon, your dad immediately wanted to track whoever did this, and he tried to call other officers in immediately. Unfortunately, that left the handling of Officer Brown to Sal, the volunteer fire chief, and two EMS workers. They brought her body to the ferry dock in order to be autopsied, but they didn't secure it properly. Thankfully, I arrived a few minutes after they did and was able to cover and protect her, hopefully sealing any usable evidence. We're working nonstop on this, boys. She's important to us and to the community overall. I promise, she will have justice."

Finally, they can speak, and all three boys start at once, creating a cacophony of voices.

Chief Fowler holds his hands up. "I understand that this is a lot to take in and that you have a lot of questions. I wish I could answer them, but I just came to fill up my thermos with coffee and change my shirt. I mean what I said. We'll work until we solve this."

Mrs. Fowler pours creamer into the thermos and then places it into her husband's open hand. He smiles and thanks her before beginning to turn toward the door. He stops again to turn and look at the boys, focusing on Avery. "Thank you for taking care of Thor and Hulk. They can stay with us unless, Owen and Landon, one of you really wants them at your house. I don't care, as long as they are still part of the officer family, and they're well taken care of."

He squeezes Avery's shoulder as he walks past, opens the front door and goes back out into the dark night.

"It's late, guys," Avery's mom says. "You're welcome to call your parents and crash here, or I can drive you home. Just let me know what you need."

Landon pulls out his phone and tells Owen he can use it in a second. Mrs. Fowler goes about getting sleeping bags and pillows while the boys look through the refrigerator and pantry for a form of dinner. Yesterday's leftovers are about to be devoured when the boys hear the front door open and see Avery's dad slip a large bag of dog food inside the door before leaving again. Avery feels a bit of pride that his dad took a moment to think of the important things; he also feels foolish for not thinking of it himself. Seriously, what kind of dog owner can he possibly be if he can't even remember food?

"Do you have a white board?" Landon's question cuts into Avery's thoughts.

"Uhh, that's completely random. What do we need a whiteboard for?" asks Owen with his mouth full of food.

"All good detectives have white boards and red string and junk like that. It's legit," says Landon.

"I'm not that bright, but what are we detecting?" asks Owen, now reaching for a scoop of macaroni and cheese.

"I just figure, we see things that our dads don't," says Landon, pushing his plate away from him. "We get to hang out more, and people don't monitor their conversations as much when kids walk into a room like they do when cops walk into a room. We're helping with the dogs, maybe we can help with the case, too."

"I mean, will they really need our help? My dad's worked on a ton of cases before," Avery says. "He'll be able to handle it."

"Yeah, your dad has done some awesome things in Jersey, no doubt, but things like this don't happen here in Summerset," says

Landon. "He doesn't know the town or the locals yet, and I'm not saying that our dads can't solve it. All I'm saying is, Officer Brown was really cool, and I just want to help."

"Plus, it'd be cool to play detective. I mean, what else are we doing?" Owen says while examining the chip he's about to put into his mouth.

Avery's not really on board with Owen's point, but he agrees with Landon. "We will have to survive with paper, and I know my mom has markers somewhere, and you can draw yourself red string," Avery says. He goes to see what he can acquire, taking his sandwich with him.

Food is scattered about the table along with markers and paper. Owen looks at Landon and says, "Okay, genius, what was your plan?"

"I say we just sling some ideas around and see what makes sense," Landon says.

"You guys are obviously going to know more than I am, but maybe I can help find any connections or holes in ideas if we talk this all out," says Avery.

"As far as I know, everyone loved Officer Brown, so why would someone want to kill her?" Landon asks in between bites of deviled eggs.

"Ummm, okay, some hypothetical situations…" Avery taps his fingers on the table and tries to think like a detective. He's watched plenty of movies. He can do this. "Did she cause any kind of problem for any of the residents, maybe not let them do something?" He looks back and forth at his friends.

Owen finally responds. "Nothing that you shoot someone over. I remember there was a thing with the Nichols family and their boat. They didn't want to leave it at the dock, but they weren't allowed to have it on property either, and Officer Brown had to handle it. Similar thing with the Andersons and a missing cat; Officer Brown said they would help but finding lost pets isn't what police officers were for. They were such punks to her about that, and you know how hard it had to have been for her to tell them no considering how much she loves these two beasts." He gestures to Thor and Hulk cuddled up under the table.

"Crime shows always say it's always the boyfriend or the ex-boyfriend, right? What happened to that guy she had been dating?" Landon asks. "Maybe he couldn't handle not being with her anymore. Or maybe he felt she embarrassed him in some way. Was she upset when they broke up? I don't think I really paid attention. I only knew about it because, you know, people around here talk."

Avery jots all of these ideas on his paper, but he agrees that none seem like a reason to kill someone.

"You've been watching Murder She Wrote with your grandma again, haven't you?" says Owen with a flat tone.

Avery ignores this. "I think the questions we need to be asking are things like why was she at the lighthouse?" he says. "Dad said things had all been routine, so is it normal for officers to be patrolling the base of the lighthouse on foot? Would they do that at the same time each night that someone would know to be waiting for her? Or what kind of crime do you guys have here that she might have just accidentally intercepted? Maybe just a family dispute gone very wrong or could it be something bigger? I mean, I assume you don't still have pirates running around?"

He looks up and sees his friends staring at him open-mouthed.

"Dude, how did you think of these things?" Owen asks with a grin. "Are you, like, a low key cop already?"

Avery rolls his eyes, though, secretly he's pumped his friends are impressed. He might not know Summerset Island yet, but he does know enough about a police investigation. He had creeped on enough of his parents' conversations and watched enough crime documentaries to at least get this started.

Landon opens his mouth to speak, seems to think again, but then goes for it, "The only problem is, what crime is there really around here? I mean, other than a few break-ins, but those shady people are always not local. So then we aren't talking about locals."

"Unless there's something going on that you guys don't know about. Is that possible?" The look on their faces indicate that it is; they obviously don't listen in on their parents' conversations like he does. "Okay, I have an idea. This is a small Southern town. You guys, like by law, have to have a little old person who knows everything about everything and everyone, right? That knows gossip both current and old school? Who is that person?"

"Mr. Bowen," Landon and Owen answer simultaneously.

"Dude, Mr. Bowen is so cool. He's a legend around here," says Landon. "He knows everything because of his surf camps. He says people just tell him stuff, but other people think he sets up microphones where the moms sit while the kids surf so he can hear their gossip."

The boys decide that tomorrow they would go see the older gentleman and find out what kind of information he has that could shed light on their investigation.

They clean the kitchen, washing dishes and putting food back in its rightful place, and then organize their notes before deciding they should probably try to sleep.

"I still think the ex-boyfriend could have had something to do with it," Landon mumbles, his face half buried into his pillow.

Avery reaches over to his nightstand and picks up the Magic 8-Ball. "Here, we can try to settle this right now. Magic eight ball, did Officer Brown's ex-boyfriend do this to her?" He flips the ball over to read Don't count on it. They all lay their heads down, and Avery tries to get some sleep, despite everything weighing on him.

Chapter 5

Mr. Bowen's house sits on the edge of the commercial district of the island. From his front porch, you can see families headed to the store to pick up their weekly groceries, people sitting outside at the coffee shop, ice cream shop, and two of the restaurants, and you have a direct view of the ferry. Not surprisingly, Mr. Bowen is seated on his porch when the boys stroll up, Thor and Hulk in the lead.

"I heard you boys have taken on the responsibility of those dogs," Mr. Bowen says instead of a greeting. "That's very kind of you. She loved those dogs like they were her babies. You know, she just had that big doggy door system installed for them and everything."

They look at this as an opportunity to go up on the porch and sit with him.

"What doggy door system, Mr. Bowen?" Landon asks once they're on the porch beside him.

"You know, she cut a hole in her back door with a flap so that the dogs could come and go as they pleased while she was at work," Mr. Bowen says. "It seemed a little strange since she had plenty of opportunities to stop by the house while she was working to let the dogs out, but the shifts are long and she did worry about them, so I guess it made sense to her. I think maybe she also worried that the new chief wouldn't take kindly to her constantly stopping by her own home while she was working, which makes sense given when she did the work. Don't worry, boy, I am not making any judgements on your father. We didn't know anything about him yet, since he isn't a local."

Avery makes his way over to the man and holds out his hand in greeting, "Avery Fowler, sir, nice to meet you."

Mr. Bowen isn't at all what he had envisioned. Avery pictured an old white-haired man with pressed khaki pants out on the porch. However, the actual Mr. Bowen is wearing his bathing suit and a Hurley T-shirt, sipping on iced coffee. A surfboard leans against the house, and salt lingers in Mr. Bowen's graying hair.

"Your father seems like a nice enough fellow. He must be really upset that town management is bringing in the State Bureau of Investigation on this and not even giving the local boys a chance at drawing any conclusions of their own. They should be here today."

The three boys look at each other, eyebrows raised.

"Oh, you didn't know that, huh? Yes, sir, Bowen hears everything. I assume that's why you're here." He leans over to pet the dogs who lay happily at his feet, not seeming to be strangers to this porch at all.

"Yes, sir," says Landon. "We were trying to think of anyone that may have had some sort of problem with Officer Brown recently, someone that would have wanted to hurt her. Maybe an ex."

"Or anything going on that shouldn't be," adds Avery. He knows his friends didn't believe that anything shady is happening in their sleepy town, but he isn't ready to rule it out.

The man chuckles, though he smiles warmly. "I'm impressed by your gumption, boys. I am sure your fathers would be proud of you for taking an interest. And you're the first sleuths that have come to me for the inside information. But the boyfriend theory, you have to let go of. You've been watching too much television. She and the ex-boyfriend were still friends, and if anyone was upset about the breakup, it was her, and not him. He's too busy trying to get his business up and off the ground to pay attention to anyone else and too stupid to realize a good thing when he loses it. At least the most recent break up; the cop she dated, there was some drama there, but that was some time ago."

"I told you, man. Chill out on the Murder, She Wrote nonsense," says Owen, rustling Landon's hair.

Mr. Bowen chuckles at the boys before continuing. "The Jacksons didn't like her too much. She busted him driving his golf cart one night when he had no business driving, and he was afraid that such a charge would hurt his reputation. Brown refused to budge, though. She didn't care about his name or his money. Unfortunately, the judge did so Jackson walked away without facing any consequences for his actions. That was hard for her. She believed there should be consequences."

And shouldn't there be, thinks Avery, if you break the law? Isn't that why people become police officers, and why his dad was away from home so much? In order to stop people from doing the wrong thing and make sure they don't do it again. Otherwise, why have police officers?

Mr. Bowen leans forward in his chair, elbows propped against his legs. "As for the shady business, well, Summerset Island has always been known for getting into a little bit of trouble. You can't have money without expecting to find it. That's what your father was brought in for, Avery, but things didn't go quite as planned."

The boys don't move, don't even blink for fear of distracting him. Avery's bent over like he's ready to literally catch every word because this was not the story his dad had sold the family on. But instead of continuing, Mr. Bowen stands up and walks to the porch railings, sets his hands down on it and looks over, turning in both directions. What is he doing, Avery wonders to himself, until Mr. Bowen turns back to the boys and motions for them to follow him into the house.

From the photos, posters, and newspaper articles displayed on the walls, Avery learns that Mr. Bowen is a native to the island, though he spent long stretches away making a name for himself in surfing contests large and small. He motions for the boys to take a seat on the couch, an oversized leather sectional, and asks if they want anything to drink. While waiting for his beverage, Avery continues to read the headlines of the various awards Mr. Bowen has won from surfing contests around the world, but also of the time Mr. Bowen spent teaching underprivileged kids to surf at neighboring beaches.

Mr. Bowen doesn't sit down this time; he stands like he's giving a lecture. "Okay, here's the thing. Summerset Island has a checkered history. They say that the lighthouse used to bring pirates from all over because we're so close to a port and the light would aid them in their hijinks. The port meant money, not just from robbing the ships blind, but those company owners and captains lived here, and their homes were lavish and filled with unique and sometimes priceless findings from their travels. The money never left, but the trouble has changed. Rumors are that our town has a problem with illegal substances, and that town management knows but has done nothing to stop it. Now that might be out of fear, and if it is, then it makes a lot of sense as to why Chief Fowler was brought in here when he was, considering his background. If he wasn't brought in out of fear, though, it seems really interesting that the man in town management that is responsible for the Fowler family's arrival has recently put his business and home up for sale."

"And by illegal substances, you mean..." Owen says.

"Drugs. Serious ones."

Owen lets out a low whistle. This was clearly not on his radar.

Avery considers all of this. Maybe the island does have a problem; it would make a lot of sense to bring his dad here after all of his experience with illegal drugs up in New Jersey. If they are trying to cover up the problem, though, they definitely would not want his father here. He would not look the other way; Avery knows that for certain. It would also be impossible for his dad to be unaware if there was a huge drug problem here; he takes his job way too seriously. Avery wonders if any of these rumors are true, and if so, could it have anything to do with what happened to Officer Brown?

Chapter 6

After thanking Mr. Bowen, the boys go on their way. There is a lot to think about.

"Okay, do we think this is legit? Or is Bowen a wackadoodle? I mean, will we be talking about aliens next?" asks Owen.

"I mean, Owen, our dads have been police officers here for years. How could they not know anything about this?" asks Landon. "That seems pretty suspect. What does this say about them as officers if they've worked here for so long and had no idea that all of this is happening under their noses?"

"You're right; they'd be trash at their jobs," Owen says.

"Or corrupt," Avery says. And enter foot into mouth. He knows he shouldn't have said it the second the words tumble out, but it was too late. All of this is so unbelievable; seriously, how ironic is it that just when his father is supposed to be leaving drugs behind, he takes over a department on an island that's home to a drug syndicate. No way.

Owen's cheeks are red, and Landon's eyes have narrowed directly on Avery. He holds his hands up, "You're right, I'm sorry; I'm an idiot. Forget I said it, please." These boys have been nothing but welcoming to him, and his dad seems to like everyone at the department. He'd notice if there is something wrong, something to be suspicious of.

"It's okay, man. You don't know our dads, and this is a pretty intense situation," says Landon. Avery appreciates his forgiveness, and though Owen didn't say anything, he lets it go, too. "I think we need to talk to them and tell them what Bowen just shared. They probably already know, but it wouldn't hurt to just play things on the safe side."

The dogs lead them back to Avery's house, where more than just his father's truck sits in the driveway. Inside, all three of their fathers, not a single one of them in police uniform, gather around the kitchen table.

"Here you boys are!" Chief Fowler exclaims. "We've been waiting for you."

Avery takes a second to get the dogs settled; he's beginning to get the hang of this responsibility thing. Meanwhile, Owen and Landon join the dads. "Well wait until you hear the tea we have for you!" says Owen.

Owen shares all that Bowen had talked about, ending with the theory of drugs on the island and how Officer Brown got hurt because of it. Avery studies his father's face, his gray-blue eyes soft. One thing that Avery loves about his dad is that he does not discredit what Avery has to say just because he is young. So yeah, this theory might be completely off the wall, but his dad will hear them out anyway.

Not all adults do that.

Chief Fowler runs a hand through his hair before speaking,

"I appreciate that you boys brought this to us. I'm aware of the rumors, and of course Joe and Brian know far more about any truth there might be to it. It's certainly something that I think we need to look into. However, I think it will just be us looking into it. Now that the SBI has been brought in, I will have very little say in what happens in the case. I'm being told that the reason they are coming is because my priority to the town is to keep the tourists safe, and I can't do that if I am distracted by a murder investigation. Plus, if we are being honest, most of the officers here are not equipped to handle that kind of investigation. What worries me, though, is that I am hearing rumblings of people believing that Officer Brown did this to herself."

The boys begin protesting and Avery's father holds up his hands in response.

"I know boys, I don't believe it either, or at least I don't want to. We have to see what the evidence shows."

Owen's father, Joe, puts his hand on Owen's shoulder, and adds, "I am really proud of you boys for wanting to find the truth for her. She would be honored to know how much you boys care. And going to Bowen, asking the questions you did, who knows, you may just end up following in our footsteps. Please remember, though, that there are professionals on the case. We don't want you doing anything that could get you hurt or in trouble."

"Yeah, but think, Dad, if you guys aren't really supposed to be investigating it, who will make sure everything is really considered? Who will care enough?" asks Owen. "At least we can ask some questions and do the leg work that the SBI won't want you to be doing, but that you know needs to be done. We're her people; we should be looking for her killers."

It's a mic drop moment.

***

Later, alone in his room, Avery lay in his bed, rolling his Magic 8-Ball between his hands and considering all that he had heard today. Officer Brown was so kind, so welcoming, always with a laugh and a smile for whoever needed it. Why would anyone think she would want to hurt herself? On the other hand, though, how crazy is it to think that Summerset Island is home to a huge crime conspiracy? "Did someone do this to her?" Avery asks.

It is certain.

Avery's eyes widen. Okay, he's clearly losing it. Sleep deprivation? Heat stroke? Stress? It's a toy, and he needs to get a grip. But then he thinks for a moment about the other questions he asked. So far, each time the Magic 8-Ball has been correct, so... he shakes his head. "Get your life right, Fowler. Go to bed," he says to himself.

***

At breakfast the next morning, he sits with his parents out on the porch and eats the eggs and veggies his dad prepared and the yogurt parfait his mom made. "Dad, I really think Owen is right. How are you guys going to investigate when the SBI knows you aren't supposed to?"

Avery notices his mother's brow furrow. She obviously agrees with Avery's dad. He told Avery and his friends yesterday that they, under no circumstances, should be involved in this investigation.

His dad sighs. "Avery, I know that you want to help, and that makes me very proud, but I need you to trust me. I will make sure this case is resolved and that she is taken care of. Right now, what I need for you to do is be thirteen. Practice soccer, get unpacked, get ready for school, take those guitar lessons you mentioned. But stay away from this case. I mean that."

Avery mumbles an okay, frustrated that his father doesn't trust him enough to do this. He can help; he is smart and brave enough. Why does it always have to come down to him being too young?

"Speaking of being thirteen and taking time for yourself, have you spoken to Matt at all since you've been here?" Mrs. Fowler asks.

"Not really," says Avery, staring down at his plate. He's kind of been a jerk; after having been so worried that everyone would forget about him, now he's so caught up in his new life that he's ignored his old friends. "I thought we'd still chat over the game, but I haven't been playing it as much."

"Yeah, I noticed. And I'm happy that you have made new friends and have picked up a new sport, but don't forget about the people who have been important to you," says his mom.

Avery nods because she's right. He's trying so desperately to fit in here in North Carolina, trying to prove he can fit in by learning to surf, he's neglecting people that he knows are around to support him, even if only from far away. "I'll send Matt an email after breakfast seeing if he wants to play tonight."

He helps his mother with the dishes before making his way to the business section of the island. He listened to both of his parents this morning, and while his mom is right, his dad is not. He won't be able to solve the case, not with the SBI here, and Mr. Bowen was right; the timing just feels all off. Avery has to at least try to help.

In order to be strategic, he rides his bike all the way to the lighthouse, taking note of the stores and shops he sees easily from the area where the horrible incident occurred. It seems that maybe five businesses total could have visibility of where Officer Brown would have been that night.

Avery starts with the closest business: the hardware store owned by Mr. Ramsey and his wife. Avery is a stranger to them both. He thinks that doing this without Landon and Owen is the wrong move. They have home court advantage, having lived on the island their whole lives, and their fathers are known and respected around town. There might only be one chance to do this, and without their clout, he might screw it all up. So Avery turns around, gets back on his bike, and flies down the quiet streets to Landon's house, thinking how nice it would be to have a cell phone.

***

"Why do we think they will help us?" Owen asks. "We're kids, not cops."

Avery found them both at Landon's playing volleyball in the pool. It stung a bit that they hadn't called him. Were they already tired of hanging out with him? He pushed that aside to tell them his plan. Well, at least the beginnings of a plan to look into any camera footage that might show who was out at the lighthouse that night.

"Our dads are never going to agree to this, but maybe if we just ask a few questions," Landon says. "They can't be too mad about that, especially if something helpful turns up."

They bike back to the hardware store. Because Landon's mom has a crazy HGTV obsession, his parents are constantly in the store, so the boys agree he should be the one to take the lead with Mr. Ramsey. A little bell chimes with the opening of the door, and immediately Mr. Ramsey, salt and pepper hair and a well-maintained beard, appears behind the counter, a wide smile on his face. "Hello, boys. What brings you in today? Picking up something for your parents, Landon?"

"No, sir, not today. Have you met Avery Fowler yet, Mr. Ramsey? His dad is the new chief of police," Landon says.

Mrs. Ramsey reaches his arm across the counter to shake Avery's hand, and they chat about the town and Avery's move before Landon gets to the point.

"Mr. Ramsey, sir, I'm just going to level with you because my father has always taught me that people value transparency," Landon says. "I know you have heard about Officer Brown. We are trying to find out what happened. Our dads have been told not to focus on the case, to pay attention only to the town and the tourists, but we feel like this is our town, Officer Brown was our friend, and we need to do this for her. We are wondering if you have any cameras set up outside your store that may have picked up helpful footage from the night in question."

Mr. Ramsey strokes his beard while Landon speaks, and continues to do so once Landon has finished with his request. His smile's gone, but his face is not unkind. "I wish I could help you boys. I think it is admirable that you want to do right by your friend. And I also appreciate your honesty and transparency. We do have a camera, though I don't know if it would have picked up anything helpful. However, even if it did, I don't think I could just hand it over to you boys. If the SBI is investigating now, that footage would belong to them; giving it to someone else, no matter how honorable the intentions, would be hindering their investigation."

Avery tries to hide his disappointment and stop himself from feeling discouraged. Then he has an idea. "We understand, sir. Do you think, though, that you could take a look at it, and if it shows anything, you could let us know?"

Mr. Ramsey gives a smile that doesn't quite reach his eyes. "I tell you what. I will look at the footage today, and if there is anything on it, I will call the station and find out who I need to speak with at the SBI."

The boys thank him for his time and then make their way back outside. Owen shakes his head, and Avery feels the way he looks.

"Hey, that is only one of five," Landon says, not seeming even slightly phased by disappointment. "We have four other chances to get some information."

Owen shrugs. "Yeah, maybe four other chances to give the SBI exactly what they need to to help coverup whatever scheme they have going on; this about what Bowen said. There's a possibility that pretty important people know what's going on. This sucks. If we were older, I bet we could have convinced him to help us. Everyone would see how sus this all really is. He thinks we're a joke. No one is going to believe us over the SBI."

"We don't know that the SBI or anyone else is up to anything. Let's just try the next place," Landon says.

But the next three places don't offer any more information. Two stores have no cameras. Mr. Lincoln, though, of the pet boutique had the same thoughts as Mr. Ramsey. He is happy to help, but he would only do so if the "proper channels" are followed. Those channels are through police officers, not the three of them.

Because they are kids. This was so unfair. Avery had a hard time keeping the smile on his face. How do people do this? Keep going after they keep getting shut down? After people who could be helping just don't? He sees Owen's fists clenched by his sides and can tell that he's ready to flip out.

When they exited the store, Owen lets out a huge whoosh of air. "Can you believe that guy?! You know Officer Brown spent tons of money in that place. She bought those stupid fancy treats for Thor and Hulk all the time, and every few weeks she was in there buying new toys. She could have ordered from the internet, but she believed in supporting the local stores. And how do they support her? Oh, yeah, I know. They don't!"

Avery and Landon stand a few steps away, allowing Owen to go through this moment and cycle through his feelings. He takes a deep breath and gives them a nod, and then the three go into the last business that might have any helpful information.

Avery recognizes Andrew immediately, this time wearing a Harry Styles t-shirt. "Interesting choice today," Avery says as he approaches Andrew.

Andrew looks down, perhaps having forgotten what shirt he put on this morning, and laughs. "Come on now, don't be hating on Harry. He has come a long way from his One Direction days. Those songs of his get caught in my head all the time. What can I do for you gentleman today? Are your drums in need of something? Or would you too like some pop star apparel?"

For the first time, Avery feels like he can handle this conversation without the help of his friends. "Actually, Andrew, we needed help of a different kind." Avery lays out their request just as Landon did at the other stores.

"Come on to the back and let's see if there's anything worth your time." Andrew walks to the door, locks it, and flips the sign to Closed. He leads the boys through the aisles of vinyl records and past the various musical instruments through the door marked private. Andrew sits down at his desk, a large oak desk furnished with two computer monitors and multiple pen holders well-organized and filled with pens, pencils, and Sharpies.

Avery wants to break the silence, talk about music or thank him, but he is afraid to distract Andrew. Avery knows how lucky they are to even have Andrew consider helping them. Andrew drums his fingers on his desk with his free hand while he scans for a file with the date in question.

"What hours are you interested in?" he asks, clicking to the right date. Owen tells him the time range, and Andrew explains how they can watch the video at a faster rate so that it won't actually take two hours.

Something happens relatively quickly, though. On the computer screen a black sedan slowly drives up, then pulls to the side of the road and kills its lights.

"Have any of you ever seen that car?" asks Avery, knowing that he wouldn't recognize a vehicle unless it belonged to his parents.

Owen leans in closer to the screen and squints. "It seems pretty generic. I can't think of anyone specifically who owns a car like this, but there are probably tons of people who drive similar ones. Then again, it's weird to see anyone driving on the island."

Avery hopes to see someone exit the vehicle, giving them something to work with. The car is still a distance away from the shop, and the way the camera is angled, two men can be seen, both wearing hats pulled low to their faces, getting out of the car and walking in the direction of the light house.

The boys keep watching...and watching...and watching. Almost two hours later the men came back from the opposite direction of which they had gone before; this time they walk much more quickly. They get in the car, pull the doors closed behind them, and drive towards the music shop camera. Andrew pauses the video as the car is closest to the camera. He attempts to zoom in, but it does nothing but distort the image, so he brings it back to its original view and Landon pulls out his cell phone to take a few pictures. Andrew lets the tape go forward a few more seconds, then pauses it again when the back of the car is visible. Landon takes a few more pictures, though again, the image isn't very helpful.

But it's better than nothing.

Andrew turns away from the computer screen to face them. "Alright boys, that's probably about as good as it's going to get with my camera. Did you already ask the other shops?"

Landon explains how they had been to the four other stores, and how there were two others who had cameras but would not give them the footage or let them see it. Owen mutters under his breath, something probably better left unsaid.

Andrew nods his head. "I get that you're upset about your dads being taken off the case. But can I ask why you aren't just trusting the SBI to handle the investigation?"

Like Mr. Bowen, Andrew seems like someone they can trust. And they had said they were trying to be transparent. Avery lets out a big breath and says, "We've heard some rumors about there being drugs on the island that the town management was aware of, and Officer Brown getting wise to it and trying to stop it. Now the SBI is here, and all of a sudden, rumor has it she did this to herself. It could be nothing, but it just seems shady."

"So, wait... if the town managers were allowing the drugs, why would they hire your dad?" Andrew asks. "That would seem like a nightmare."

"That's what I keep trying to remind these two," says Landon. "We have no proof that anything is wrong with the investigation. Right now, it just sucks that our dads can't help."

"I get that," says Andrew. "I liked Brown. She was always kind, and she even brought me a donut every so often. She wasn't just a good officer, she was a good human, so here's what I can do to help. I will look back in my footage and see if there are any other times that car or one that is similar comes by. Maybe I can get a better look at the guys or their license plate."

Avery's eyes open wide because he's been hit with an idea. "Or maybe you can notice a pattern, of when they are around, and then we can tell our dads when to expect them next. Would you have the time to do that?"

In an equally pumped tone, Landon adds, "Or if you don't have the time- and if you don't mind- I'm down to do it. I am pretty good with computers, and I have nothing but time."

It's decided, then, that Andrew will give Landon a quick tutorial on how to use the app, and then Landon will watch as much footage as he can from the last two months, which is as far back as Andrew's back-ups go.

"Sweet," says Owen, "But can we eat lunch while this is happening?"

Chapter 7

Avery and Owen walk toward the sandwich shop to pick up lunch for the four of them. As hungry as he claims to be, Owen stops them.

"Whoa, what are all those trucks doing there?" asks Owen.

There are a number of black SUVs outside the police station, far more than what Avery has seen before. Owen and Avery decide to check it out. Avery pulls the door open and sees that his father isn't in his office. The secretary nods her head in the direction of the conference room, where Chief Fowler, two other officers, and a handful of men in suits sit around the table. The chief's lips are in a tight line and his brow is furrowed. The secretary then nods to the seats by her desk, only steps away from the conference room. Avery smiles at her gratefully.

Through the closed door, the boys can still hear the raised voices from within. Avery hears a voice he did not recognize say the words "according to the doctor, it could have been a self-inflicted wound." Avery hears his father's voice raise over all the others, "You, sir, did not know this woman. I did. There is no way that she would have done this to herself."

Murmurs and grunts, then suddenly the door is thrust open. When Chief Fowler walks out of the room, he signals to the boys to follow him into his office.

Though he has only officially been in the position for a few days, the chief has added a few personal touches to help the space feel more like his. Avery recognizes the glass bowl of assorted stress relieving balls and gadgets from his last desk, and he sees the picture of his parents on their wedding day. He can't help but think how pretty his mother looks with her long brown hair and the ivory dress with little purple flowers. His parents didn't have a large wedding. His mother's favorite place had always been the beach, and his father was happy to do whatever she wanted. He married her on the beach, toes in the sand, wind in their hair. And now they get to live at the beach; maybe his dad's decision to move was mostly about his mom and making her happy. She hated his old job, the hours, the risk. Next to that is a picture of Avery as a toddler napping on the couch with his dad. Avery wonders how often that happened and wishes he could remember the times when his dad was around to do things like that.

The chief closes the door behind them but doesn't sit in his chair or offer them a seat. "What's up, fellas? This isn't really a good time." His voice isn't cold, but Avery can see that the warmness that is usually in his dad's eyes is gone right now.

"Dad, did the SBI really just say that she did this to herself?" Avery asks, knowing that his dad will be irritated that he could hear the discussion through the door. "That this wasn't a murder?"

Chief Fowler exhales loudly and adjusts his watch face. "Look, they have it in their heads that the doggie doors she installed make it seem like she didn't intend to come home again."

Avery interrupts, "That makes no sense, though. I mean, you all were at her house within hours of what happened. The dogs weren't left alone any longer than they normally would have been. She knew that everyone knew about her dogs. She knew no one would leave them alone."

"I know, son," says the chief, "which is why we are fighting against it. Again, I just need you to trust me and to stop listening outside closed doors in a police station. So, what can I do for you? What brought you in?"

Avery stammers an excuse about seeing if he wants lunch. His father thanks him but tells the boys that he is about to go meet someone about a case. "You boys have fun. I've actually gotta run now, so I will walk you out."

"Oh, Dad, I kinda forgot Landon's order. Do you mind if I use the phone here to call him and check it?"

"Sure, bud. Just make your call and then head out, okay? I will see you for dinner." Then he leaves the office.

"Dude, I remember Landon's order," Owen says. "No need to call him."

Avery shoots him a look. "Yeah, man, I remember it too. I also remember Landon having a theory about police department conference rooms. Maybe if we can sneak in there, we can see what they know already."

"Ahhh, I gotcha. Let's get in there then," says Owen as he

walks right out the door and over to the secretary, Maggie. Avery is really worried about what Owen without a plan looks like.

Owen smiles wide at Maggie. "I'm sorry to bother you, Maggie, but Chief told Avery to grab his keys, and they aren't in his office. Do you mind if we look around the conference room to see if they fell out of his pocket or something?"

There's no way she falls for that, thinks Avery. But somehow, she says yes, and the boys rush into the room. Just like Landon had said, white boards fill the space. If only Avery had a phone to be able to take pictures of everything, so they could get in and out as fast as possible. They will just have to read what they can and hope to remember it.

Avery scans one white board while Owen reads another. They have barely been in there for a minute when they hear Maggie's voice. "Did you find them?"

The boys look across the room at one another. It's a small space. Staying any longer will look suspicious. They both walk out of the conference room, shrugging their shoulders.

"Guess he must have lost them earlier this morning. Oh well. Thanks, Maggie!" Owen says before heading out the door and back into the sunny day outside.

The sun is pounding down on them, radiating off the asphalt of the parking lot. Avery feels like he's sweating to death, and it probably isn't from the sun, but the fear of getting caught. He doesn't want to make his dad look bad or get in trouble himself. Too bad he didn't think of that before he snooped around the conference room with Owen.

"What are the odds she tells my dad we were in there?"

"Who, Maggie?" asks Owen. "Nahhh. She's cool. She won't say anything. So, what did your board tell you?"

"Something important, actually. There was no gunshot residue on her hands, according to the medical examiner."

Owen lets out a loud whoop and starts jumping around the parking lot. "That proves it! She obviously did not shoot her gun."

"I don't think it's as easy as that," says Avery. "According to the board, she was wearing open tipped gloves, so it is possible that she wouldn't have any residue. What did your board say?"

Owen rubbed the back of his neck, and Avery can already tell he doesn't want to share what he read. "So, I guess Officer Brown had a history of emotional instability according to her parents. They had a doctor's name written up there, one who lives on the island. It said she suffered from anxiety, whatever that means."

Anxiety means the fear of leaving your home and having to make new friends but realizing that maybe they don't like you as much as you think they do and failing to figure out why. It's worrying that your dad doesn't know you, or doesn't like you, or isn't proud of you, or maybe just won't make it home. It's the need to know and control what can't be known and controlled, Avery thinks to himself, but he doesn't say it. Maybe he wouldn't seem cool if he did, and he really needs to seem cool so that Owen and Landon like him.

"Well, I guess we know more than we did, so good on us," Avery says. "Let's go get lunch."

"You don't have to tell me twice."

They begin walking in the direction of the sandwich shop, the one that makes their own chips which are ridonkulously good; it's only about two short blocks from the police station. Avery's still getting used to how close everything is. "Man, it's sweet to just be able to walk anywhere you want to go. I'd have to wait until my mom was available if I wanted to go anywhere other than my friend Matt's house. It sucked. I guess the bad side is that you don't have a lot on the island, huh?"

"I mean, no, but we can live without a McDonalds. There are benefits to being here that other places won't come close to," says Owen.

"For sure, for sure," Avery says, worried he's said the wrong thing again. He's distracted by the thoughts in his head.

A few moments pass. "Dude, is that your dad?" asks Owen.

Avery looks up to see that his father is walking a little ahead of them on the sidewalk. Then, out of nowhere, Chief Fowler breaks into a sprint, shouting ahead for someone to stop what they are doing immediately. Avery starts running, Owen right behind him, but it isn't until he stops that he understands what his father is upset about. Around the base of the lighthouse stand a few large white tents, the kinds used for big events. Chairs and tables have been assembled; a DJ is currently setting up his station. The crime scene tape has been torn down, and a man with a hose in his hand is rinsing away any residue of what had occurred just a few nights ago. There is no going back and re-examining the crime scene. The crime scene has been erased.

Chief Fowler walks at a brisk pace towards the tents, his eyes set upon a man in a yellow polo shirt tucked into his jeans. "What's going on, Dennis?" the chief yells. Owen leans over and whispers to Avery that Dennis is the town manager. Anything that happens in Summerset Island goes through him. The boys stay a few feet away. The sun beats down upon them, tourists mill around the lighthouse before they would be asked to leave for the day's private event.

"I told you, Fowler, I need you focusing on the town, not this investigation. Murder doesn't happen on Summerset. The men here are not able to handle a case like this; for one, they don't have the experience, but they also don't have that kind of mindset. It takes a certain kind of person to be able to investigate murder," Dennis says.

"No, Dennis, it takes a police officer. Maybe that is the problem; you don't seem to have enough of them. But I am a police officer, and I should have been given access to this case. The medical examiner had inaccurate information on the report. Now, you have allowed the crime scene to be ruined. Why would you do that? This is an officer's life," Chief Fowler has a pleading tone in his voice on those last words.

Avery recognizes his father's point: is money really more important than her life is what he is asking. The answer should be no. The answer should always be no. Avery thinks Dennis seems a little embarrassed as he said his next words, "The island needs money in order to run, Fowler. And these weddings bring in a lot of our revenue. I couldn't cancel it, and no one wants a crime scene in their wedding photos."

Avery's father leans in close to say something, probably not complimentary, before turning and seeing Owen and Avery. He says nothing, though, and Avery realizes he and Owen better get those sandwiches pronto.

Chapter 8

Landon is still working away when Owen and Avery return to the music shop with food. He doesn't even stop working to eat, and Avery feels useless just sitting around. He helps Andrew with a new window display, but Landon is still at it, so Owen and Avery go outside for Avery to learn how to juggle a soccer ball. Owen has amazing control over the ball and can get an obscene number of touches. Avery looks like an uncoordinated baby deer in comparison. Great, yet another thing for him to practice.

Andrew kicks them out at closing time, "You don't have to go home but you can't stay here," and Avery heads towards his house alone. From a few houses down Avery can hear the sounds of his dad's frustration. When he walks into the house, his father is wailing on the drum kit, one of his favorites from the Foo Fighters, and Avery hangs out in the kitchen with his mom so his dad can have his space. Afterwards, his dad seems a little more at ease, and the family sits down to eat the meal Avery made with his mom.

"Hey, Dad, I've been thinking that maybe I could swing by Officer Brown's house and grab a few things of the dogs. Like their beds and toys, and whatever treats they like. I mean, Thor and Hulk live here now, so shouldn't they have their stuff?"

"Well, you can't be swinging anywhere," says his dad. "The SBI still has it closed off as a crime scene. However, I can ask for permission to acquire the dogs' items. I'll make a call after dinner and if they okay it, I can drive you so you don't have to drag the dog beds behind your bicycle."

The SBI officer leading the investigation gave permission as long as the only things that Avery or his father even touched were related to the dogs, and, to be on the safe side, they sent an agent to unlock the door and monitor.

Walking into the house feels wrong, Avery thinks. There are so many colors, so many pictures, the house obviously belonged to a woman who was happy, who believed in making memories with the people she held important. He walks into the kitchen to get the dogs' food and notices a pad of paper with a to-do list on it written in Officer Brown's handwriting: buy laundry detergent, pick up heartworm pills for the boys, change the oil in the truck, pick up prescription, and get price estimate on new shocks from the Firestone in Southport. A few of the items on the list had check marks next to it, the others were obviously meant for her to complete when she was off duty the next day.

Do people who plan to not be around make to-do lists? It doesn't seem likely to Avery, but he is not an expert on this. He has to admit, he isn't even an expert on Officer Brown; she had just been really nice to him, and he wants to make sure justice is served for her. After finding the many dog toys Thor and Hulk have, piling them in a basket, and loading the beds into his dad's truck, they go back home to help the dogs get settled better. The two have been sleeping horribly, whining and crying at night, seeming to know that something is wrong and probably missing their owner.

Avery sets up the two dog beds in his room for now, wanting for the dogs to feel comforted by his presence and by their bedding. They go for a long walk on the beach, and back at the house Avery gives them the treats they like and scratches behind their ears for a while, until they seem willing to relax. He looks at the time and realizes that he's a few minutes late to meet Matt in the game.

His mom is reading on the couch, and he feels a little bad about interrupting her, but his room currently is without a television. He powers everything up and types in his log in information, and then his dad stands directly in front of the television.

"Ummm, Dad, I'm not sure if you've heard this before, but your father was not a glassmaker." His mom uses that awful joke often enough, and it serves them right to have to listen to it now.

"Not the time for jokes, kid. So, I lost my keys today, did I?

Crud. How did he find out? Would Maggie have said something? Or did Owen tell his dad, and if he did, what did he say? Avery will admit to wanting to snoop, but he didn't come up with the way into the room. These thoughts fly through Avery's mind, along with panic because his parents are staying quiet and that's never a good sign, but also worry that he can't trust Owen, that maybe he threw Avery under the bus. Avery doesn't want to throw any shade on Owen if this is only coming from Maggie, though.

Ugh, being thirteen shouldn't be so hard, he thinks.

Play it cool. "Oh, did you? Bummer." Avery keeps his eyes on the screen, or what he can see of it.

"Avery, I've already told you to stay out of this case. How is it going to look if you get caught snooping around sensitive information? I'm supposed to be able to control a whole town, but I can't control my own son? The town won't trust me to do my job. Can you understand how important this is?"

Avery didn't think anything about his dad getting into trouble, and now he feels like a punk. Because obviously, if people realized what Avery and Owen did, it would make both of their dads look bad, but his especially.

"I'm sorry, Dad. I didn't think. We just wanted to help."

"I get that, bud, but I've been doing this a long time," says his dad. "I just need you to give me time and space to do my thing, okay?"

"But you're not allowed to. The town brought the SBI in, and what are they doing?" Avery yells. "They are letting the crime scene be destroyed and accusing Officer Brown of doing this to herself, and she's not here to defend herself. And what does it say about the department if she did do this?"

"You're not wrong to be concerned, but you need to stay in your lane. I can't talk about all of the details of the case. I can't tell you what I do and don't know and what I am going to do about those things. It comes down to trust, kid. And trust goes both ways, Avery. You're not showing me that I can trust you. Maybe a night without your video games will remind you of that."

"But Dad, I emailed Matt and made plans to play together tonight! It's the first time since we've moved that I was going to talk to him. I've got to get on here."

"No, Avery. You've got to listen to me," says his dad before leaving the room.

Avery's mom has been sitting on the couch the entire time, not saying a word. She's still cuddled in the corner of the sectional with the book in her lap. Avery looks at her and wonders if she'll let him play. She is the one that told him to reach out to Matt. He opens his mouth to ask her, but she speaks first.

"Don't even think about it. Your father's not happy, kid, and I don't blame him. You can use my phone to call Matt. That's as good as it's going to get," she says.

***

He tried to explain to his mother that most teenage boys don't sit on the phone and talk, but it didn't work. Matt stayed on the phone for about ten minutes and asked for pictures of the dogs and the house. Avery told him about his dad catching him in the lie, and Matt asked if Owen was responsible or if they were actually friends. *If only I could know for sure,* thought Avery.

With nothing else to do, Avery decided to organize what he did know about Officer Brown. It doesn't matter to him what the SBI says; someone did this to her and the answer has to be out there somewhere.

On the one hand, there is the radio call saying that she had three people that she was dealing with. That would be incredibly suspicious to any officer, as it was the middle of the night. If it had just been kids, Avery didn't think she would radio that in. Instead, she probably would have just told them to go home, maybe called their parents, if not then, the next day. Also, who were the two men they saw on the camera footage? They were in the vicinity of the lighthouse around the time the shooting occurred; no businesses would have been open, so they had no reason to be out by the lighthouse at all. Avery needed to find out who those two people were, and then where is the third person? Avery continued the list with the fact that there is no conclusive evidence that she fired her gun. The fact that she had a to-do list for the next day, the fact that she loved her dogs as though they were her children, and that everyone seemed to consider her a good officer, good person, or good friend, makes it seem unlikely she would do this to herself.

The State Bureau of Investigation feels that the doggie door system is a sign that Officer Brown did not plan to return home. The lack of gunshot residue does not mean that she didn't fire her weapon because she was wearing gloves. And, what no one has said but should be pointed out since he's exploring all angles, she easily could have faked the scenario of three people over the radio.

Avery sits back and reads through his lists again. There has to be more information to find, though it will be hard to find it thanks to the lack of a crime scene. When he climbs into bed, he picks up his Magic 8-Ball, thinking of the right question. If only it could just give him a name or tell him something real. He stares at the ceiling for a few minutes, hoping the right question would come to mind. Instead, he falls asleep.

Chapter 9

Avery wakes up to the sound of his dad talking to the dogs. He is sitting on the floor, back to the wall, allowing each dog to rest its head in his lap while he rubs their ears. He is telling them that today is going to be hard, and they need to be on their best behavior. Today is Officer Brown's funeral.

"Hey, bud. How are you doing?" Chief Fowler asks.

Avery sits up, his hair going in multiple directions. He wipes the sleep from his eyes and gives a slight, short smile. His dad nods. They don't need to say any more about it. Avery goes over to sit by his dad and the dogs, who are now licking like crazy and rolling on their backs for attention. They deserve it; today they will be saying goodbye to their owner. Avery finds bowties that Officer Brown had purchased for them, probably for a wedding in the past, and puts them on the two dogs before getting into his own suit. His mother helps him with his tie, and when his father comes into the kitchen, she ties his too. Avery laughs and his father asks what is so funny.

"How is it that you know so many things, but you can't tie a tie?" Avery asks between bites of Captain Crunch.

Now his father laughs, and his mother smiles.

"Your father knows how to tie a tie. He just lets me do it because it gives me an excuse to be close to him." Avery knows he should be grossed out at this moment, but he likes that his parents are so happy together. His dad puts the leashes on the dogs, hands one to Avery, and the family walks together to the church for the service.

The walk is not incredibly short, but as the chief had assumed, the parking lot is packed. Squad cars from departments near and far filled the spaces of the church and the neighboring businesses. The church, more of a chapel, is white but pristine. The town spends money on its upkeep due to the number of weddings held here each year. The steeple rises high into the air, seemingly touching the clouds, standing out against the bright blue of the day's sky. There isn't enough room for everyone inside, but people congregate outside, the sun beating down on them.

Officer Brown's sister, Megan, walks up to the pulpit and looks over the heads of the rows of guests. She clears her throat, the echoes of that heard throughout the silent church.

"Many of you only refer to Diana as 'Officer Brown.' You have lovely stories about her chasing those dogs of hers around or times when she was able to help you. She was always so happy to help. But I never knew my sister as an officer. To me, she was always just Diana. The wild one who wasn't afraid of a thing in the world. When she was five years old, she found her way to a stage the first time, and even though she just had a small role, everyone was talking about her at the end. That's how big her personality was. Of course, this made her incredibly dramatic as she was growing up. Everything was going to be the end of the world." She pauses to let the crowd chuckle.

"But if anyone could handle those challenges, it was her. I remember when she was fifteen, the tiny thing she was, not up to most of our friends' shoulders, marching right up to my ex-boyfriend and punching him in the nose for breaking my heart. And even though she was tiny, she knew how to pack a punch. That fierceness, that love for her family and friends, it never faded. She loved this island. She cared for all of you, and she wanted to keep you safe. She would have punched each one of your ex-boyfriends in the nose if you needed her to."

There's laughter, but that's not why Megan has stopped speaking. Her tears have gone from occasional to overpowering. She takes a deep breath.

"She somehow saw the good in everyone. And she would be so grateful to see you all here today. I know my family and I are comforted to know that the town she loved so much loves her back."

She returns to her seat, making room for her uncle to approach the microphone and talk about how Officer Brown would never be forgotten, how she was always the brightest light in the room. The priest calls for other guests to step forward, and many do, including Avery's father who speaks about how it was her emails that convinced him to take the job; she was so kind, so eager to learn, and she loved the town so much.

A folded American flag is given to her parents in respect for her service, and the congregation leaves the church and walks to the burial site. On the way, Avery listens as people tell their favorite stories about Officer Brown, stories about how she dressed up as a superhero and put her dogs in capes and went to the preschool and read to the kids. Stories of her having stuffed animal drives to donate to police stations so that children who are in scary situations will have a comfort object in a moment when they need it. Stories of her chasing geese off the lawn of the lighthouse on wedding mornings. Andrew tells of how she cried tears of joy when the town threw her a surprise birthday party. Mr. Bowen mentions how she was a person of integrity and how rare that is to find these days. And when everyone has said all that there is to say, dispatch calls her badge number over the police radio frequency.

"7260?" A pause.

"7260?"

The last call. There are very few dry eyes. Avery notices the black ribbons hanging around trees in her honor. He wonders how long they will be there, and if the town manager will get rid of them in the same rush that he got rid of the crime scene. Avery hopes not.

Chapter 10

Avery meets up with Owen and Landon at the cafe. He orders a green smoothie for himself and is pleasantly surprised when the girl behind the counter passes him biscuits for the dogs, too. Orders in hand, the boys go out to the patio. Avery's list sits on the table, but it's neglected because the boys aren't talking. It is more interesting to eavesdrop on what other people are saying.

At the table behind them, a group of older women discuss the possibility of a killer running around the island. "How scared should we be? We've never even had to worry about locking our doors before, and now this?"

Another voice says that the SBI isn't ruling it a murder. A third said, "This is selfish, but I would rather that be the case. It's terrible to think that may have happened to her, how scared she must have been. I don't want to be that scared; I don't even want to have to worry about it."

"And think about what this will do to property value! Summerset Island having a serial killer roaming the streets. And what is that new chief doing about it? Is he even old enough to have this job?"

Avery's face turns red at that comment. He wants to turn

around and say something to those women, something about how amazing his father is, not just at his job, but in general. Say something about how the town manager is the reason things are so ridiculous, the reason that there is no clear answer as to what happened. Maybe even ask them what they know about the rumors, men being out in the middle of the night, and these modern-day pirates. However, he sits in silence. When he can't listen to it anymore, the three boys get up and walk over to the music shop so Landon can watch more of the video. He has to find more proof. It is their only hope at this point.

Avery helps Andrew with inventory. While they work, they discuss bands that they like and when Avery could begin taking guitar lessons. Owen is throwing the ball for the dogs out back behind the store. After about an hour, they hear a whooping from the office, loud enough that even Owen hears it outside. Avery and Owen, from opposite directions, come rushing into the back room to hear about the excitement. Landon is leaning towards the monitors, speaking quickly about how he strategically tried to scan each image, but Avery isn't hearing the words. He needs to hear what Landon found, not how he found it.

"Check this! Every third Thursday, this same black car makes an appearance around 1a.m. But that's not the exciting news!"

"No, that is exciting, Landon. This means that our dads know what to look for and when!" Owen interjects, his smile wide.

"That's possible. But it's also possible that those guys will change their pattern after what happened. I mean, they didn't just shoot anyone. It was a cop. That's a big deal," Avery says. He shares Owen's excitement, but he doesn't want to get his hopes up too high.

Landon turns to face his friends. "It's okay, though, I was able to get the type of car and the first two letters on the license plate. Our dads should be able to use that, or the SBI should be able to. This should give them a lead!" Sitting on the screen of the computer is the image of a Nissan Altima and the first two letters of the plate, LS. It is a standard North Carolina plate, the beginning of the phrase "First in Flight" glaringly obvious.

Avery, Owen, and Landon all wear matching smiles. "Avery, call your dad," says Landon.

But that is where the excitement ends for Avery, and his smile fades. If he calls his dad right now, he will know that Avery has been doing exactly what he was told not to do. Yeah, technically it was Landon, but Avery knows his dad will be angry. So as much as he wants his dad to be proud of him for working hard on something and finding important clues, now, less than twenty-four hours after losing video game privileges, is not the time.

"I can't." Avery explains about his dad calling him out last night for the lost keys incident.

"Awww, man, what a bummer!" says Owen. "I really didn't think Maggie would spill. I wonder if your dad is going to say anything to mine."

At least Avery now has the comfort of knowing that Owen did not rat him out.

"So what do we do with this?" Landon asks. "Or was it all just a waste of time?" His brow is scrunched, and his mouth open in disbelief. Avery understands his frustration and thinks for a minute.

"Hey, Andrew, could you maybe email it to my dad, not mentioning anything about us?" asks Avery.

Andrew had been quiet this whole time, mostly trying to get his own work accomplished while the three boys set up shop in his store. "Sure, but I gotta be honest. I already sent the footage to the SBI, so it's possible your dad already has this information. However, if they are icing him out, then this will be really helpful to him."

Of course Andrew sent in the video footage. He probably didn't have a choice; the SBI probably demanded it. But Avery felt better knowing that now his dad definitely has access to it, and he has to hope his dad can find a way to make it useful while also not figuring out that Avery had anything at all to do with it.

***

Things finally feel like they might turn around, and Avery relaxes. Today is the day of the soccer game Officer Brown had given Avery tickets for, and he wants to focus on it and enjoy it for her.

Avery has never been to a soccer stadium before. He knows it won't be like watching some of the major teams on television, but it is still an impressive sight. The expanse of the field, bright green, vivid, luscious grass, goes on and on. Outlining the field are banners highlighting the local team's wins from previous years, state champs, southeastern regional champs, eastern regional champs. Next to those hang the banners for retired players, their faces now looking over the field they once dominated on. Each player's stats are proudly presented, and Avery considers the likelihood that he could ever be as good. He imagines asking his Magic 8-Ball later, and the answer returning something like an outlook not good. He decides to practice more.

The boys find their seats: first row, right behind the bench.

"What do you think Officer Brown had to do to get such amazing seats?" asks Landon. "We will be able to hear everything the coaches and players are saying while we watch the game!"

Avery's mom made sure he had enough money for food, drinks, and even a t-shirt if he wanted one. And he did, because now he realizes how serious the fans are, especially those sitting in the section he's in. Avery walks over to the stand with foam fingers, posters, and souvenir jerseys and buys himself a blue and white striped jersey just like the other fans have. He also grabs some mini pizzas and bottles of water for him and his friends, so they won't have to miss a minute of the game.

"Sweet shirt, Avery, and thanks for the pizza. Or I guess, remind me to thank your mom," Owen says while opening the personal pizza and watching the steam escape from the open lid.

The boys eat their food while they watch the introductions and announcements that precede the game. The players run onto the field and do some last-minute warmups and stretches. Some come over to the stands and high five those sitting close enough to reach. The coach walks over, stands directly in front of Avery and his friends, and says, "Which one of you is Avery Fowler?"

In a hesitant voice, confused as to why anyone here would know who he is, Avery responds, "I am, sir." The coach turns in his direction, smiles, and sticks out a hand for shaking.

"It's nice to meet you, Avery. I'm Coach Rivenbark. Officer Brown told me a while ago to keep an eye out for you; she said you were new to the area and were really into soccer. No disrespect to any of your fathers, but Officer Brown was one of the best police officers I have ever known. She was kind, she cared for the people and the town. This was her home, and she was one of the few people that truly treated it like home. You probably didn't know this, but she was also a huge Hammerheads fan. There were very few home games that she missed. In fact, when she was younger, I was her high school coach. Considering everything that's happened, and that she had a special interest in you boys, the team and I decided that you should sit on the bench for tonight's game. Those are the best seats in the house if we do say so ourselves."

Avery looks out to the field, at the players leaning in to give each other pep talks or talk strategy, some are stretching, some just seeming to take in a moment of relative quiet before the game begins. And he is going to experience it right alongside them! The three boys scramble to say yes and thank you and this is so amazing and everything all at once.

The coach laughs and tells them how to get down to the field, and then he meets them down by the gate and opens it for them. As they walk over to the bench, Coach Rivenbark points out a few of the players. They sit down on the bench, a few players saying hello before they make their way to the field.

The game begins, the local boys staying wide, effortlessly turning seven or eight one touch passes into opportunities to score. The strikers take command of the field, barreling through the defense and taking every opportunity to score.

Avery is amazed at how the men work together. It isn't about making sure an individual looks good, or one person hogging the ball, it's as if each player owns their corner of the field and the team trusts each individual to do their job. His team back home did not function like a team compared to these guys. He watches as a wing heads the ball towards a center, the keeper dives and stretches his fingers and arms as far as they could go, straining his every muscle, the forward driving across the field with the speed that made it seem as though there couldn't possibly just be one of him. The ball is volleyed across the field with strength and intention. Avery wants to learn how to do that.

As they come off the field, the players take turns explaining the strategy, why they hold off at some moments, "See what he's doing there? He's waiting for them to gain speed because it's easier to catch him off guard," kind of explanations throughout the game. When the victory is secure, a two to one win, the players shout and cheer along with Avery, Owen, and Landon, allowing them to run on the field with them. The athletes find Sharpies and sign each of the boys' shirts.

"Thanks for being fans," Coach Rivenbark says as they turn to go out the gate and follow the stream of spectators still exiting the stadium towards the parking lot.

"Mom, you won't believe how amazing tonight was!" Avery shouts as he opens the door to her Jeep. The boys clamor in, excited to share their stories about the amazing night. She waits until they have all gotten settled and buckled before pulling away, despite how long it takes due to their enthusiasm. Their smiles last the whole way back to Avery's house, where they are surprised by the living room set up being completed. The television is now mounted with the cable hooked up, including the channel that plays professional soccer games all day, every day.

Mrs. Fowler makes the boys big bowls of ice cream and lets them shout at the television while watching Liverpool take on Manchester United, a game from years ago. When Chief Fowler gets home, he sits with the boys for a few minutes and listens to the play by play of their night.

Owen mentions that the school has soccer clinics beginning in a few weeks, though he doesn't know when sign-ups for that started or ended.

"It probably wouldn't be a bad idea for you to sign up, Avery," says his dad. "It's been a few months since your season ended, and I can't remember the last time you practiced."

Heat rushes to Avery's cheeks, and he inwardly thanks his father for calling him out in front of his friends. He's been busy, with the move and then everything that's happened since. All he's wanted to do is show his dad that he's good at something, and here's a reminder that maybe he isn't.

"Dad, do you think if I go by the school tomorrow someone would be there to talk to about it?" Avery asks. He knows his dad could just make a phone call or two, but his dad's wearing deep circles under his eyes these days thanks to the stress. This is something he can do for himself. After knocking on the doors of strangers and learning how to surf, he is feeling pretty confident. His dad agrees it's worth a try, and if not, he will make a phone call.

After that, Chief Fowler pushes himself out of his chair. He is walking more slowly than usual, the weight of everything obviously sitting on his shoulders. He says goodnight to the boys. Mrs. Fowler pops her head in the room to remind Avery to let the dogs out again before they call it a night. "Oh, and if you want to wash an ice cream bowl or two, I won't stop you," she says before saying goodnight.

"Is it just me, or do our parents look a little older after these past few weeks?" asks Owen. They are all sprawled out on the floor, each in their own sleeping bags. The dogs have taken over Avery's bed and lie curled up together, happily panting after being let outside for a quick run around the back yard. Owen currently has the Magic 8-Ball in his hands and has entertained himself by asking a variety of ridiculous questions, like whether he will captain the soccer team this year or if Elizabeth Prince will give him the time of day this year. The answer to that is very doubtful, which causes Landon to laugh until tears fill his eyes.

"Man, she is so out of your league. Try at least sticking to girls in our grade, though even then you might have a hard time," Landon says through his laughter. Avery laughs now, though he has no idea who this Elizabeth Prince is and why she is out of Owen's league. He assumes she is probably out of his league, too.

Owen tells Landon to shut up, "Like your game is any better," which quiets Landon pretty quickly.

Owen passes the Magic 8-Ball to Avery, who asks, "Will the information Landon found help our case?"

"Wow, way to kill the vibe, Avery," Owen teases. Avery didn't mean to ruin their fun, and he definitely doesn't want Owen or Landon thinking he's lame. He can't help it, though. As much fun as tonight is, it is only thanks to Officer Brown.

"We owe tonight to her. Don't get me wrong, I had a great time, and Landon did an awesome job with the video footage, but there's got to be more we can do, and I am not ready to walk away." The other two boys agree to that, and Avery finally looks down at the toy in his hand.

You may rely on it.

Avery thinks for a moment and asks another question, "Will the town now let our dads help in trying to find the truth?"

Don't count on it. Avery's mouth falls into a straight line.

"That can't be right, can it?" Landon asks, while rolling over to prop himself on his elbow. "I mean, those guys out there so late, at the same time she is out there? If anything, they had to have seen other people out that night or heard something like their voices, even if they weren't involved."

"No, you're right, Landon, but the problem is going to be finding them and then making them interested in cooperating. They were out in the middle of the night," says Owen. "Somewhere else, that is probably no big deal, but here? What are you doing in Summerset Island at 3 o'clock in the morning here? My guess, nothing good." He still stares up at the ceiling, and Avery wonders if he thinks it might hold the answers.

Avery considers what his friends have said and then looks again at the toy in his hands. He shakes the Magic 8-Ball and asks, "Were those guys caught on camera part of this crime?"

It is decidedly so is what appears when Avery flips it over to get his answer and Avery reads it out loud to his friends. "You know what's weird, guys? I haven't gotten a single wrong answer from this thing yet. Everything so far has worked out like it has predicted."

"But it also said you weren't ready to hear the truth about the town council, which just seems like a cop out," Owen points out, finally turning his attention from the ceiling. "You can't really think that a piece of plastic could actually have the ability to predict the future." He looks at Avery flatly, and Avery realizes how silly it sounds.

"We could always test the theory," says Landon. Owen and Avery both sit up and turn to look at him. "Ask it something about tomorrow. Like will your mom make us pancakes for breakfast, or will we hear good news at tomorrow's press conference. Something where we can get answers fast to compare, and maybe more than one question so that we can really see if the hypothesis is accurate."

"Wow, you are such a nerd," says Owen. "How did I never see this before?" He flings himself back against his pillow. Avery, however, thinks it seems reasonable. Scientific evidence, just to test it, just to check.

His parents very rarely eat pancakes. His mom loves them, but they usually stick to eggs because of the protein and health benefits, which irritates Avery because he loves pancakes. He looks at the Magic 8-Ball and says, "Will my mom make pancakes for us tomorrow morning?" He feels confident that the reality tomorrow will prove to be negative.

Most likely. Owen must be right. This is silly.

However, it doesn't hurt to ask one more question, so he asks about good news at the press conference tomorrow.

Outlook not so good. The boys now look at one another, seeing it as ominous despite the fact that a minute ago they were calling it a toy.

"This is stupid. Tomorrow will be fine. The SBI has to take a look into that information you found, Landon. That's a toy. It will be fine," Owen says before rolling over to face the wall. Landon and Avery exchange looks, but they lay back too. Nothing else is said that night, the only sounds were the whirring of the fan, the breathing of the dogs, and the distant beating of the waves upon the shore.

Chapter 11

Avery wakes up to Thor's hot, slobbery tongue exploring the expanse of Avery's face. "Ugh, thanks, Thor, but please stop, buddy."

This does not stop Thor; in fact, all it does is invite Hulk over to join in on the festivities. "No, no, no," Avery chants, now waking up his two friends. They laugh as they watch the two dogs mal Avery's face, but their laughter stops when the dogs turn their attention to Landon and Owen. Avery makes his escape to the bathroom to wash his face, multiple times.

After the boys have all had a chance to clean the slobber off of themselves and dress, they grab the leashes from a hook Mrs. Fowler put up specifically for them. They strolled into the sunlight, the day already warm, the world already alive and boisterous. Dolphins make their way through the water in the distance, pelicans dive into the water for their breakfast. The day is beautiful.

They forget about time as they walk the dogs and turn back because Owen's stomach growls so loudly the sounds of the ocean can't even mask it. When they open the back door to Avery's house, Mrs. Fowler is making breakfast in the kitchen. Avery asks the question even though he can clearly see the answer for himself, "Mom, what are you making?"

She pauses what she is doing, putting the spatula on the counter so that she can pet the dogs who have grown very attached to her, and smiles in greeting to the boys. "I know, we haven't had them in forever, but it felt like the kind of morning that needed pancakes. Your dad has already left, and you know he prefers French toast, so I thought I would take advantage of his absence and make my favorite. I put berries and chocolate chips in them too."

Mrs. Fowler turns to the sink to wash her hands before resuming her pancake preparation, and while her back is to them, Avery, Landon, and Owen, all wide-eyed and open-mouthed, exchange flabbergasted looks. They did not see this coming.

"What are the odds?" Owen mutters under his breath, prompting Mrs. Fowler to ask what she missed.

"Nothing, Mom. We were just taking bets last night on what you would make for breakfast, and Landon had guessed pancakes. I'm surprised that I lost," Avery explains as he went to the sink to wash his hands. He pulls down glasses from the cupboard and takes orange juice out of the refrigerator.

"Oh, well, lucky guess, right? Will one of you feed the dogs? These will be ready in about three minutes. Good timing getting back from your walk," Mrs. Fowler says, putting her concentration back to the griddle in front of her while Landon goes to do as she asked and Avery sets the table. Owen collapses into a chair, and Avery can hear him mumbling, "It is a coincidence, obviously." He can't be too upset because when Mrs. Fowler puts a plate of pancakes in front of him, he digs in, content to enjoy the food and let everything else go. While they eat, Mrs. Fowler asks about their morning plans of going by the school and reminds them about the press conference, as if they could forget.

After they clean the kitchen, the trio rides their bikes over to the middle school. Owen explains there is no reason to lock up their bikes today; no one else would be coming by the school. Inside the front door is the office, bustling even though no students are on campus. A woman with curly blond hair looks up from her computer screen and smiles. "Ahh, Owen, Landon, how are you boys? And who do you have with you? Let me guess. You are Avery Fowler."

Small towns. It's still pretty creepy. He smiles at her respectfully and nods.

"Hey, Mrs. Morgan. We're doing okay. We were hoping Coach was in today. Avery didn't know about the clinics coming up in a few weeks, and he would like a chance to go. Do you know if Coach is around?" Landon asks.

"He sure is. You know where to find him." She sends the boys away with lollipops, and they laugh about it when they are far enough away. But Avery thinks to himself that he will never be too old for a lollipop.

Landon explains that Mrs. Morgan is the one that Avery will end up talking to if he has issues with his schedule and also about attendance. "Well, that won't be an issue. My parents have never let me miss a day of school in my life," Avery grumbles. "And since my mom will be working here, she surely won't let me skip."

"Tell me about it," says Owen as he gestures to the left. "This way." He knocks on a door that is labeled with an athletics department sign. They hear a garbled "Come in" and push the door open. Sitting behind a large, very disorganized desk is a tall man, maybe in his mid-twenties with shaggy hair and sunglasses on his head. The stacks of papers on his desk seem unsteady, and Avery does not want to get too close in fear that he might knock them over. The plaque on the desk reads Coach Gilmore.

Owen and Landon both say hey to the coach before introducing Avery. The coach reaches over his desk with the scary stacks of paper and shakes Avery's hand. "Yeah, your dad called me a few weeks ago. Midfielder, right? I'm sure Owen and Landon have told you we're ready for some fresh blood on the team this year. We had quite a few eighth graders leave, so plenty of slots to fill. As long as you are willing to work, to try, we will get along just fine. I just ask that you really show up for us each time you are on the field."

Avery stands up a little straighter and says, "Yes, sir, I can do that."

The coach smiles and says, "That's exactly what I needed to hear. So what brings you boys in today?" Avery explains about the clinics, and how he didn't know about them but would really like to participate so that he can be in good shape for tryouts and hopefully the team overall by the time the season begins.

"This isn't about just being able to hang out with your two buddies here, right?"

"No, sir. I really do want to see how I can grow this year." He thinks about how incredible the game was last night and how much it means to him to have his dad in the stands.

"I like the attitude, but usually we have people tryout prior to clinics so that team members get priority time in the stations they need. How soon could you come in?" asks Coach Gilmore.

Avery feels the eyes of everyone on him. His father's words ring in his head; it has been a while since he practiced. Is he good enough to make the team? He was decent enough on his last team that he always got a little bit of playing time, but what if that isn't good enough here?

He swallows hard and says, "I can come in whenever." He crosses his fingers that whenever is not right now. He doesn't want Landon and Owen to see him choke.

Coach passes Avery a clipboard for him to fill out his name and contact information. "Okay, how about Monday? I need your parents to fill out and return these forms, too, and then you will be good to go. But be ready. These try-outs are legit. It is not just a formality."

Avery thanks him, feeling overwhelmed and unsure. He hopes that it isn't obvious by the look on his face. How will he be able to keep hanging out with these guys if he doesn't make the team? It will be beyond embarrassing; he might as well ask his mom to start homeschooling him. He can already hear the smack

Owen will talk.

Coach Gilmore tells them to go enjoy the next few weeks because he plans to work them hard once the clinics begin.

With the school behind them, Avery looks at his watch and realizes they better head to the town hall for the press conference. They hop on their bikes and pedal furiously, hoping to make it there before it begins.

***

A podium is placed in front of the entrance to town hall, a microphone in its center. No one stood behind the podium yet, but despite how many rows of seats had been placed out that morning, not a single chair sat empty. Avery tries to scan the crowd for his father, hoping that a look at his dad's face will tell them what to expect, but he does not see him. Realizing they have no chance for seats, the boys walk their bikes over to the ice cream shop where an empty bike rack sits before finding a good place to stand underneath a large oak tree. The shade is a benefit to having to stand.

They plop on the ground and listen to the chatter around them. The voices that trusted that the police would keep them safe, the ones that said the Summerset Island police force isn't qualified or competent enough to protect the town from a killer, they all ricochet around the crowd. Gossip makes its way through the rows of people about how Officer Brown was so unhappy, while other people suggest that the town is dirty and everyone is okay living as ostriches with their heads in the sand so that they could keep their nice beach and big houses. Some people begin to raise their voices, as if the louder they speak the more important their words become. It is all a blur, all this noise, all these faces, most of which Avery doesn't recognize, some whose names he still has not learned. He wonders what it must be like to be Owen or Landon, to see these people who babysat them as babies, sat with them for over a decade in church, handed them ice cream cones or chicken fingers, fixed their air conditioning units, now all acting this disunified. It must be discombobulating.

Dennis, the town manager, finally appears from the town hall building. People begin to silence themselves, waiting for him to speak. Camera crews move in a little closer. Dennis lingers at the microphone; papers are in his hands to guide him, but he hesitates, opening his mouth and then closing it again, staring out at the crowd and all of their questions. Either way, people would have something to say. If it were a murder, people would be frightened, and if they ruled this as an accident or something that Brown planned herself, her friends would rush to her defense. There is no winning.

Dennis clears his throat and looks out over the crowd. "Hello everyone. I am so glad to see you all today, despite the reasons for which we are gathered. I know there has been much uncertainty over the past few weeks. Many of you have felt frightened and felt unsure of the security that has always been provided for you here in Summerset Island. This island is a place for families. It is a family. We work together, we know each and every one of our neighbors' names, their children's names, their grandchildren's names. We help each other in the garden or run little errands for the woman next door whose children are holding her hostage, sometimes literally."

He pauses for the brief laughter that comes here. People are smiling in response to his words, appreciating the description of their home. "We take pride in each other, in our businesses, in our homes, in our island. And the event that occurred a few weeks ago should not change that, should not discourage you or shake your pride and your faith in this community."

It's a sea of nodding heads. Avery is beginning to get impatient. Say what we are actually interested in hearing, he thinks. Scanning the crowd again, he sees his father, hat pulled down low. It isn't police issued, it's the same one he uses when they go hiking or to the beach, army green and worn on the bill; it's his favorite. He's not smiling.

Dennis clears his throat again. "We all loved Officer Brown. She was an amazing police officer that responded to every call with urgency and efficiency. It didn't matter what the issue was, if you needed an officer, if you needed her, she was there. If she couldn't help, she got you the help you needed. She will never be replaced, and she will always be missed. A plaque will be put up in her honor on the exterior of the police station so that we will never forget.

"As you know, the State Bureau of Investigation was brought

in to handle this case. The town, not the police department, felt that this is the best way to ensure that there is no bias, no oversight, and no interruption to your daily lives. We, the town council, felt that this was in the best interest of every person on this island. Unfortunately, there were many interruptions to this case. After discussing things with the State Bureau of Investigation, we and the county prosecutor's office feel that there is no foul play. They, the SBI, are satisfied that the bullet came from her own gun, as well as by her own hand."

Gasps were heard, sharp breaths drawn in. Some utter phrases of relief. Avery feels no relief. He feels suspicion and distrust and looks again to his father. His dad's jaw is clenched and tight, his eyes laser sharp on Dennis, who continues speaking.

"Many factors led to this conclusion. Unfortunately, no witnesses were identified, and despite our requests for people to come forward, no one has. We must assume that she was out at the lighthouse alone that morning. Without witnesses, it is impossible to build a list of credible suspects. I think we can all agree it is impossible to imagine Officer Brown making any enemies. Interviews were conducted with her family, friends, ex-boyfriends, neighbors, and even acquaintances; anyone that could have been considered a suspect was spoken with. Yet it led nowhere. Finally, according to an SBI crime lab forensics test, the bullet did come from her own gun. It does not seem likely that she would have put herself in the position for someone else to harm her with her own weapon."

Rumblings from the audience again have Dennis pausing. Many people don't buy that kind of wound is likely to be self-inflicted. More people do not believe that Officer Brown was capable of wanting to hurt herself.

"People can debate this as much as they like, but the SBI itself has pronounced this type of wound to be possibly self-inflicted. We may not want to believe this, but we can only work with the facts that we have been given," Dennis says. "Her firearm was moved from its original location, disrupting the crime scene and possibly destroying evidence. Then, due to the need for that area of the island for an important event, the crime scene itself was wiped of any forensic evidence. Her body was quickly moved. Perhaps if even one of these things had not happened, maybe we would have found a lead, had a question answered. Again, with the facts that we have, a homicide does not seem likely. This decision was not made quickly or lightly. All facts were considered. We are saddened at the thought that one of our own would have struggled so much, been in so much pain and felt so alone. As you leave today, I urge you to take one of the pamphlets we have created about grief and depression, as well as what to do when you are feeling these things. You are not alone, and the town wants you to know that we support you. Free counseling will be offered throughout these coming weeks, but we are always here for you."

Dennis opens the discussion to questions from the media only, but the boys didn't need to hear any more. Avery and his friends turn their backs and begin walking to their bikes. Avery clenches his fists; he is so discouraged at what seemed so obviously wrong and unfair.

Landon keeps his eyes on the ground, his hands in balls by his side. "All that time looking through every frame of footage. I bet they didn't even use it," he says, his voice barely above a whisper.

Each boy has his hands firmly on his own handlebars, and each looks down at his own feet. There is really nothing that they can say to one another, nothing that can lighten the mood or inspire a laugh. It's over, and it isn't justice.

Chapter 12

Avery sits on the steps of the back porch, throwing the ball for the dogs with very little enthusiasm. His family has just had dinner, and he can see his mother and father at the sink, talking and laughing as they finish cleaning up the kitchen from the meal. He wonders what they could have to be so happy about after today. When he looks up again, it's just his mom he can see in the window by the sink. His father steps out on the porch with a cup of coffee in one hand and a water bottle in the other. Despite all of the available chairs, he sits next to Avery on the steps, puts the water bottle by Avery's feet, and then puts his arm around his son.

"It's not over, bud."

"Dad, you have obviously had one too many cups of coffee today and it is affecting your brain cells. I was at the same press conference as you. It seems pretty over. Maybe if they hadn't brought in the SBI things would have gone differently," Avery's voice trails off. His father already knows everything that he can say.

"The SBI was coming in regardless. That isn't a town decision; any time there is the loss of an officer, it is their job to come in and investigate," says Chief Fowler. "What is different in this case is that the local police department was shut out of the investigation. But I'm not closing the case, yet. Maybe I am wrong, maybe it is nothing, but I can't just let it go. She may have only been one of my officers for a few days, but I won't do that to her."

He takes a sip of his coffee and stares out to the distance, watching the waves as they beat the shore, though Avery isn't sure that his dad is really seeing anything other than the thoughts running around in his head.

They sit for a time in comfortable silence, both existing with their thoughts. The dogs seem to realize that no one would be throwing the ball again, and they lie down by the two sets of feet.

His dad clears his throat. "How'd it go with the soccer coach today?"

Avery explains about having to tryout on Monday and about how nervous he is.

"I get that. It's a new school, new coach," says his dad. "But it's probably just nerves. Do you want to grab the ball and practice for a while?"

Avery really did. But he couldn't bring himself to practice. Not today, after everything that happened. He didn't want to bring it all up again, though. "No thanks, Dad. Not tonight. I'm super full."

"Yeah, between dinner tonight, and I heard there was a pancake extravaganza this morning. I can't remember the last time your mom made those."

"That's because you like French toast," Avery mumbles.

"Yeah, it's a superior breakfast food, just accept that fact and everything else that I say, right?" says his dad. "I taught you to like Legos and wrestling and camping, so I know good things. Anyway, take tonight off. But I think we should practice together."

They go back inside, and Avery's mom suggests that they watch a movie and settle down. His parents let him select the movie, but he goes with one that he knows his parents like because they watched it together on one of their first dates, Clue. It was apparently considered old even then, but his mom made his dad watch it.

"Don't we have enough mystery on our plate?" Chief Fowler asks, but Avery doesn't see it that way. He watches the movie now because it's funny.

"Besides, Dad, at this point we all have it memorized. There's no mystery left there," Avery says. The family settles onto their sectional couch, each of them having a place that they consider their own. Chief Fowler sprawls out in a corner, Mrs. Fowler leaning into his side. Avery lies with his head by his mom, knowing that every so often during the movie she will stroke his hair like she has since he was a baby. Since it is just the three of them, Avery doesn't have to act like he hates it or that it embarrasses him. The movie makes them all laugh and brings a sense of comfort to Avery.

Later, Chief Fowler takes his turn walking the dogs before bedtime. As Avery waits for their return, he looks at the list and the papers he has accumulated over the case of Officer Brown's death. He writes a list of each of the town council member's names, using his laptop to search the website for that information. He adds what businesses they owned and how long each had been a member as well. He did not think that any of them would have had any type of grudge against Officer Brown, but obviously in life, accidents happen. This could have been an instance of wrong place and wrong time. He picks up the Magic 8-Ball to ask about each of them individually, but he stops to consider if there are negatives to that. What if the ball is wrong? What if it leads Avery to follow someone that has nothing to do with anything, and then other clues are missed and erased, as so much evidence has already been, because he followed a lead that a toy gave him.

But maybe a question or two wouldn't be so bad. "Can we trust Dennis?"

As I see it, yes.

Well, at least that is a relief. Avery thinks before shaking the Magic 8-Ball again and asking his next question. "Did the SBI use the footage from the music store?"

My sources say no.

He doesn't know whether to be angry or relieved. Is the SBI guilty of sloppy police work or corruption? Or maybe it's late and he's letting a toy dictate his emotions. He just wants the truth. It seems like since he's moved, there have been so many questions and very little answers. He's tired.

Chapter 13

Avery wakes early thanks to Thor and Hulk. They began bounding around the room when Avery's father was in the kitchen making coffee, relentless for attention, or food, or just to get outside and use the bathroom, who knows, but they would not stop until their desires were met. So instead of sleeping, Avery picks up his surfboard and walks down to the shore. The water is cold the second it hit his toes, but he pushes through, knowing it will warm up the longer he is out there. He sits on his board, bobbing up and down like a buoy, content to just feel the power of the ocean around him. He watches younger children splashing around in knee deep water, their mothers in chairs only a few feet away. The kids seem happy and weightless, underneath the sun and loving every minute of it.

He turns his attention back to the waves, popping up on one just a few minutes later, waiting for the moment it begins to bend, to fall apart so that he can feel as though he is gliding over the water, the power of the water his to weave and control for a few moments.

When he has had enough, he rinses himself and his board in the outdoor shower his mother recently installed for him. As his father predicted, she is not a huge fan of all the sand being tracked into their house. He secures his board on the back porch, and his mother passes him so she can go for a run, still nervous about him being on the beach without parental supervision despite the fact that his father explained repeatedly that teens basically ran wild on the island as long as they stayed out of trouble. In her defense, there was just a murder so staying close to home is pretty important.

"Alright, bear, I left you a plate of eggs with various veggies and proteins on the counter. Wash your plate when you're finished. Call me if anything happens, or leave me a note if you head out."

He thanks her, but it turns out to be for nothing because when he opens the back door, he sees someone else eating his breakfast. "Hey, Goldie Locks, seriously? Doesn't your mother feed you breakfast?" Avery asks with a twinge of annoyance. He is hungry, and Pop Tarts don't sound as filling.

Not even bothering to clear his mouth of food, Owen responds, "Hey, my mother loves me. I am her pride and joy, the reason she lives and breathes, so of course she feeds me. But finders keepers or whatevs. I am a growing boy maintaining this physique." He flexes quickly before picking up the fork again and shoveling in more food.

"I'm sorry, I must have missed the physique bit. What am I supposed to see there?" Avery taunts.

Owen responds with a flat look of irritation. Avery knows that sports and fitness mean a lot to Owen. While Landon seems to shine behind computers with his brain, Owen is the brawn. Or he is trying to be. But where does that leave Avery? He's certainly not trying to fill the role of beauty. More adjectives need to begin with B.

While Avery is irritated to have his breakfast eaten, it is nice to see his friend, who obviously feels so comfortable in his house, he just came over. It's just like Matt used to. "Did my mom let you in before she left?"

"Nope, I just came right in. You guys really should lock up around here. I mean, we think there is a killer on the loose. That's not smart on your part," Owen says while he slides off the stool and walks over to the refrigerator in search of something to drink. Avery gives him the side eye. He has never had a friend feel that comfortable and needed to make a mental note to remind his parents to lock the door. He doesn't want to tell Owen that he is not welcome, but he also doesn't want to have to worry about his breakfast in the future. He is hungry.

But also, why are his parents leaving the door unlocked? They never would have in New Jersey. He guesses they really are settling into small town life.

Avery decides to just grab a smoothie on the way to the police station, this way hopefully saving some of the food in his house from being devoured by Owen. After stopping in his room to change, Avery pulls Owen out of the kitchen and out the front door, locking it behind him. They decide just to walk to the station, kicking a soccer ball between them as they go. Avery tells

Owen about his exchange with the Magic 8-Ball last night.

"Dude, you know it's a toy, right?" Owen asks. "The whole pancake thing... it proves nothing. Don't be cray."

"People didn't think that electricity or airplanes would be a thing over a hundred years ago, but things happen, magical and amazing," says Avery.

"Really, you are trying to make a connection between your plastic toy psychic and the invention of electricity? You really must be losing it, man," Owen laughs.

"No, all I am saying is that sometimes things happen that some people can't explain. Sometimes you just need to have some faith in the world around you," Avery counters softly. It is hard to argue Owen's point. It is indeed hard to believe, but Avery isn't ready to give up hope yet. They go back to kicking the ball back and forth as they walk, the roads empty of passing cars and lined with flowers and palm trees.

When they make it to the Smoothie Shoppe, Owen stays outside to practice juggling the ball while Avery goes to get his drink. He waits in line, trying to see if he can guess the difference between a local and a tourist, anything to keep his mind busy and distract him from the length of the line in front of him. Before he even moves three places in line, he feels something cold bump his arm. Avery looks up to see Andrew passing him a green smoothie. "You looked like you needed this sooner rather than later," Andrew says in response to Avery's thank you.

Today, Andrew's t-shirt proudly bore the faces of the members of Nirvana. "Do you have any shirts without bands on them?"

Andrew laughs, but his answer is serious, "I have t-shirts of all kinds, but very few bands can contend with this one. I would think you'd be all about them. Dave Grohl was their drummer before everything happened with Kurt and Courtney and craziness, and now he's the guitarist and vocalist for Foo Fighters. That could be you if we get you in for some guitar lessons."

Avery admits he didn't know much about Nirvana, but he promised to rectify that by coming by the store later and picking up an album.

"Fair enough. How are you doing otherwise?" asks Andrew. "I heard about the press conference."

Avery just looks down at his feet. Andrew claps a hand on Avery's shoulder. "Yeah, I thought as much. Another reason why you needed a green smoothie. Come on, let's get out of here." He leads Avery out the door, beverages in hand, and into the gleaming sunshine. Avery plans to walk with Andrew to the music store, but Owen tells him it will need to wait a minute.

"While I was standing out here, I saw a swarm of news vans drive past. They're on their way to the police station," says Owen.

Andrew says he will see them later, and Owen and Avery run in the direction of the station. Even from a distance, Avery can see the vans surrounding the front of the department. The press conference was yesterday, so what would they possibly be doing here today?

"Does this happen often?" Avery asks Owen.

"No. Usually the island only makes it on the news when the town is trying to bring in more tourists or when something happens on the beach, like a drowning or shark," says Owen. "It has nothing to do with the police station."

Reporters were staring intently into the cameras in front of them, each angled so as to avoid the other. The boys pause to hear what is being reported. The closest female anchor stands with her camera facing the light house instead, a somber look on her face.

"Just weeks ago, Officer Diana Brown was found dead at the base of Summerset Island's famous lighthouse," she says. "Many of you have followed along in the investigation of her death. Just yesterday, town manager Dennis Wilkins held a press conference letting the community that knew and loved Brown know that the State Bureau of Investigation ruled her death a suicide. While there are many who claim this statement to be impossible, what is possible is that we will never know the truth, especially since evidence from the case has recently disappeared. Authorities will not confirm what items exactly have gone missing, but various sources have confirmed that the evidence room here at Summerset Island Police Department was broken into, and items from the Brown investigation have disappeared. This is an unfortunate beginning for new Police Chief Fowler, whose reign here at Summerset Island began the same day Brown died. Will this be how his time here ends?"

Owen lets out a low whistle. Avery doesn't even know how to respond. Does this have something to do with what he and his friends were doing? Did he somehow get his dad in trouble? All he wanted was to make his dad proud. And if it has nothing to do with Avery's actions, maybe Mr. Bowen was right all along. Maybe someone isn't happy that Chief Fowler is there, and maybe this is how he will be forced to leave.

Avery and Owen make their way into the station, and Owen heads straight for the place where donuts should be. Sadly, there are none. Officer Brown is no longer there to make sure everyone gets their sugar fix. "This is a travesty," he mumbles. It is, but not because there are no donuts. Avery can see his father at his desk, the phone up to his ear. The two make eye contact, and Avery's father waves Avery towards the office. He quietly opens the door and quickly slips inside so that his father will still be able to hear whoever is on the other line.

"No, I have been waiting on hold for Detective McFray. It's really imperative that I speak with him regarding his recent case in Summerset Island. Yes, I will hold again," Chief Fowler says. He sits with a stiff back, ignoring the back of the chair completely. It doesn't look comfortable, but this is his dad's working position. It is not about comfort but efficiency; the chief doesn't understand people who don't do their jobs, Avery knows because his dad has ranted about it far more than necessary. From the look on his face, he obviously also does not understand people who cannot answer the phone.

Avery stares at the large painting that is newly hung above his father's head. His mother's initials are in the bottom corner, but Avery did not see her paint this. He realizes that he has not been paying much attention to what she has been doing since they arrived on the island. He assumed just unpacking their house, but she must have accomplished more than that, because here is a painting of Avery out in the surf with his board, his father leaning against the gate watching him. There were pinks and oranges still in the sky as the sun still found its way up to the sky, gulls flying in the distance, and an expanse of turquoise water out past some dunes and beach. Neither of their faces were in it, but Avery had the sense of what his mother is trying to show: Avery growing and trying new things and his father not too far away, there both to help and cheer him on. Something that would not have been the case in their last home.

Avery's dad covers the receiver with his hand to be able to say something to Avery. "This is an important call, bud. Are you okay?"

"Yeah, Dad, I just came to check on you."

Avery's attention is brought back into the room as his father's voice slices through his thoughts, "Yes, sir, thank you for taking my call. I have a question about the Brown case that you and your team closed this week. The investigation in general is a little awkward for me as we were not asked to take part in it."

His father pauses, listening to the booming voice of the other man. Avery can hear words like thorough and extensive coming through the phone. The man sounds irritated that someone would call to question the case and mentions Officer Brown's family and something about insurance.

"I am sure they have plenty of questions about that, but I am not calling on their behalf. I am calling for my own piece of mind. I knew her, I have men that have worked beside her for years and they cannot believe this has happened. I tried to get a copy of the report, but the administration office said that it could take weeks to get all of it organized and available for public consumption. I am hoping that my men and I are not considered the public, considering everything."

Avery begins fiddling through the stress relievers on his dad's desk, trying to seem as though his attention is fixed on the bowl and not at all on trying to eavesdrop on the phone call. He's getting little snippets of words. Was that a name? Did he say the letters from the license plate?

Another pause before Chief Fowler thanks the man on the other end of the phone and says he'll be looking for the report.

"So, you just came by to say hello?" his dad asks, voice filled with suspicion.

"Well, no. Owen saw the news vans go by, and we wanted to figure out what was going on. We overheard from one of the reporters that evidence went missing. Are you going to get in trouble for that, Dad?"

"I'll be honest, kid, I don't know what's going to happen about that," his dad says. "But whatever it is, we will be okay. You don't need to stress about it."

"Well, what'd they take?"

"What'd I just say? Avery should deal with Avery things while I deal with my things. Don't you have guitar lessons today? Why don't you head that way to keep yourself out of trouble?" His dad stands and walks over to the door, opening it for Avery.

Avery turns back to look at the painting again and says, "Mom did a really good job on that."

"She's incredible, your mother. Tough as nails but soft as a marshmallow," they chuckle together at that. "Keep out of trouble, and I'll see you for dinner, kiddo."

They walk out into the common area together. Most of the desks are abandoned, on duty officers on patrol in the town instead of hiding in the air conditioning. Maggie looks like she is doing her best not to strangle Owen, who has taken it upon himself to keep her company while he waits for Avery. He pulled a chair up to her desk and has his feet propped up on her desk. She seemed only to be partially listening to him explain his plan for soccer this year when Chief Fowler says, "You do know this is a business establishment, right Owen?"

Owen sheepishly takes his feet off the desk, his cheeks a little more pink then they had been a minute before. Avery would have felt bad for him if Owen hadn't stolen his breakfast this morning, so instead he laughs, and his laugh brings Maggie to smile too. "Aww, don't worry, Owen. I enjoyed hearing all about your plans. It's good to have goals, just remember that you have to focus on school too."

Owen droops a little at her comment; he looks at Avery and

asks if they are ready to go.

"Yeah, let's pick up some donuts and head to the music shop," Avery suggests, and the promise of sugar makes his friend brighten a little.

***

Armed with a pink box of chocolate frosted donuts, Avery and Owen open the door to the music shop, sounding the bell that alerts Andrew of their arrival.

"We come bearing donuts," Owen shouts, not bothering to look to see if he would disrupt any customers with his bellowing. Other than Andrew, though, the store is empty, but Landon's head pops out of the back, his eyes looking weary but a big grin on his face.

"Hey, what are you doing here, Landon?" Avery asks, genuinely surprised to see his friend here.

"I couldn't let it go. I've been going back through everything to see if there is any other time that car shows up on screen," says Landon. "Andrew's been a second set of eyes between lessons and customers. That car never makes an appearance, though. Only those Thursday nights."

Avery opens up the box of donuts and pulls one out for himself. He takes a bite and enjoys the chocolatey sensation before forcing himself to consider the options of what Landon is saying. "Well, that could mean two things, right? One, most locals never use their cars. They have golf carts and bikes, or they just walk.

Maybe we don't see the car in any other frame of footage because it belongs to a local, and he or she only drives in the middle of the night. Which would be strange, but then again, I wouldn't want to wander about in the middle of the night either because people can be creeps. Or the other option is that whoever's in the car, whether they own it or not, doesn't live here." He takes another bite of his donut, and another, until he devours it. Landon pushes the box toward him, having already consumed one himself.

Andrew pops his head in the door and offers, "Ahh, your dads would be so proud. Not even real detectives and already putting a hurting on an innocent box of donuts!"

Avery and Landon just keep chewing, but Owen shakes his head and says, "That's so overdone, man. We know, cops like donuts. But you know what, all humans like donuts. They make people happy. I feel very happy right now allowing the sugar to course through my veins. You will have to try harder than that to get under our skin."

This causes Andrew to laugh a little harder. "Seriously, Landon, I think it's amazing that you've taken the time to do this. The attention to detail, the meticulousness of your work... but other than looking in everyone's garage, how will you find who you're looking for?"

Avery wants to scream in frustration because Andrew is right. They can't do anything with this information, other than sneak out of their houses on the next Thursday night, but what good would that do? Here they are again, with information in their hands they are too young to do anything about. Avery wishes he could talk to his dad about it, but he already knows what his dad will say. To be patient and to trust him. He does trust his dad, but maybe it's everyone else he doesn't trust. Them and time, because it seems like it's running out.

Landon looks miserable, his mouth in a severe frown, the light in his eyes gone. Avery imagines how this must be for him after spending so much time. He also feels a little bad; after all, Avery started them down this path, and look where he has gotten them. Absolutely nowhere. How stupid was it to think they could pull this off? He hopes Landon isn't upset with him.

"Landon, I guess since you've been here, you didn't hear about what happened at the police station?" asks Avery.

Landon shakes his head, his eyes still glued to the computer screen.

"Apparently some evidence went missing, though my dad wouldn't tell me what it was."

"And that, my dear Avery Watson, is why it pays to be chummy with Maggie," says Owen, kicking one leg over the other and crossing his arms behind his head.

"Alright, Owen Sherlock, spit it out," says Avery, shoving another donut in his face. He can't help it; they're so good, and he's still hungry.

Owen leans forward in his seat, excitement oozing out of him. "Well, I sat by Maggie really just to run my mouth and kill some time."

"No, not you," interrupts Landon.

"Rude much? So anyway, I was my usually charming self, asking Maggie about her potted plant collection and whatever, when I noticed a stack of pictures on her desk," says Owen. "They were evidence pics, and it was real obvious what went missing. Officer Brown's uniform boots, the ones she was wearing when she was killed."

"Who would take her boots? And why?" asks Landon.

"And how would they take them? Where has the evidence been stored? Do you guys know?" Avery asks.

"There's an evidence room in the back of the station," says Landon. "It's really small, more like a closet, but there is very rarely any evidence to be collecting around here."

"Landon, do you think you can hack into the security system?" Owen asks, his voice amplified with excitement. He's out of his chair, ready to do... something.

"Whoa, whoa, whoa," says Andrew. "I don't think it needs to come to that. Your dads will have access to the security footage. They can handle it. Come on, Avery. It's time for your lesson."

"Just one more thing. Does the name Asiago mean anything to you?" asks Avery.

"Dude, that's a kind of cheese," says Owen. "What are you talking about?"

"My dad was on the phone earlier with an SBI agent. I heard the guy mention a Dr. Asiago, and I remembered that you had mentioned Officer Brown had seen a doctor."

"Oh, Dr. Amando. Yeah, this is why you're a Watson still and not a Sherlock. What about the doctor?" asks Owen.

"I couldn't make out anything other than the name, but maybe whatever he said to them had the SBI rule her death a suicide," says Avery.

Owen and Landon exchange a look; Avery can't tell if they think he's a dodo bird or a genius. He'll have to figure it out after his lesson.

Avery follows Andrew out of the office. The front of the store has a bay window that allows plenty of natural light, and today two bright red stools are in the store's window and propped up against the stools are acoustic guitars. Avery doesn't know much about guitars, and when he asks Andrew what type these are, Andrew responds with, "Irrelevant. You could learn on a toy guitar from Amazon if given the opportunity. I didn't pick these guitars because of the brand, but because they are twins of each other and most others, so if you can get comfortable with this guitar, you should be comfortable on most other ones, or at least acoustic guitars."

They both sit on a stool, guitar in their lap. People walk past the window, chatting and smiling, finishing their ice cream cones, the sunlight highlighting everything. Avery feels like he is on display for the whole town, and it made him a little nervous. "Don't be nervous. We won't actually be playing today. Today, you will learn the names of the various parts of the guitar. You'll hopefully learn how to hold it properly."

Avery tightens his grip on the neck of the instrument. "Like this?"

"Still no, but that's cool. It's why we're here," Andrew says. "We'll talk about the names of the strings and maybe how to tune the instrument. No one out there will hear you make that baby purr like a dying cat. No worries. An added benefit is that it gives you a great view of the town and everyone coming and going. Or any type of car you might be looking for."

Avery takes his eyes off the guitar and looks directly into Andrew's face. "Have you seen the Altima around?"

Andrew shakes his head. "That doesn't mean anything, of course. But Landon is making himself crazy over this. I think you guys need to come up with something to do and let your dad handle the license plates. He's got the info, he will be able to make something happen because he has resources you guys don't have."

"I'm sorry if Landon has been in here stressing you out. It's hard to focus and enjoy other things, though. I mean, we did go to a game..."

Andrew cuts off Avery's line of thinking. "I didn't mean to distract yourselves. I mean, what's the next step of your investigation?" Great question. "Think about that while we discuss the anatomy of the beautiful object in your hand."

Avery spends an hour with Andrew discussing machine heads and fret boards, their jobs, string types, and placement. Avery doesn't play a single chord, as Andrew promised, but he does build his interest and his respect for the instrument.

Unfortunately, the Altima never makes an appearance. An idea does formulate itself in Avery's mind, though; when he, Owen, and Landon left the music shop, he doesn't walk in the direction of his house. His friends follow behind carrying on their conversation about who is the better soccer player, Pele or Maradona. Owen argues that it can't even be compared without looking at their entire teams and shouting out "GOAT" every so often. They do not realize their destination until Avery stops on the sidewalk in front of it.

"Dude, what are we doing here?" asks Landon as he stares at Officer Brown's yellow bungalow. Her azalea bushes out front are in desperate need of watering, though the grass is freshly cut, probably by a neighbor who didn't want to deal with the eye sore. The back gate has been left open, no longer a big concern because the dogs are not there to escape. Avery walks to the gate without saying anything to his friends, hoping to get out of the road before a neighbor realizes they are there.

"We're getting some of our own answers," says Avery. "Look at the porch; there is no police tape. Was there ever? Did they ever really go through everything before finalizing their investigation?" He is now in the backyard looking around. In a perfect world, there would be a key hidden in an easy to find location. This is a small town, after all. He lifts potted plants and sifts through rocks to see if one has a false bottom.

"What answers do you hope to find in her landscaping, bro?" asks Owen, leaning against the back porch and all around not being observant or helpful.

"I'm looking for a key, obviously."

Landon goes to another corner of the yard to see if he can find a spare key, and eventually Owen wanders over to some trees, where, not surprisingly, he comes up empty handed. Avery's frustration grows; he thinks he could probably get a key from a neighbor, make a claim about the dogs, but he wants to be able to do this on his own. Not because he has aspirations for burglary, but because after only Andrew was willing and able to help them with the video footage, Avery doesn't have much faith in the neighbors being willing to help.

About to give up, Avery finally takes note of the garden gnome. It's of a dinosaur devouring tiny gnomes. His mom has the same one, with a key hidden inside it. He picks it up and examines the bottom, barely breathing. The bronze key immediately glimmers once the sunlight finds it, like a treasure finally seeing light after years of being buried. "Jackpot," Avery whispers as he picks it up, slides it into the door handle, and turns. They are inside.

Chapter 14

"Now what's the master plan?" Landon asks, his voice not as confident as it could be.

The quiet is good, though. Avery can't get caught breaking into Officer Brown's house. He will be grounded like he never has before. He won't have to worry about soccer tryouts. He won't be allowed to play, surf, or see the light of day again. It's a huge risk. It is a risk he's willing to take, though.

Avery doesn't know what they should be looking for, but he hopes he will if and when he sees it. "Look for anything that seems important, I guess. Things that might show that she had plans to come home or maybe something that indicated she was worried about someone. Maybe a planner or a, what is it called, not a diary but a..." he trails off, not really trying to come up with the word because he thinks that they get the point. "Whatever we find, let's try to be fast. We don't know if anyone saw us come in."

Landon moves with intention toward the living room, calling over his shoulder that he is looking for her laptop. If the SBI investigated at all, they would have taken the laptop as they swept through. Everything seems untouched, though, waiting for Officer Brown to return. Avery walks through the kitchen, hoping something will pop out from the pristine white cabinets. He opens a few of them, but other than not being very organized, nothing stands out as suspicious. Nothing that his own parents' kitchen doesn't have. Next to the refrigerator hangs a white board calendar. She had written things on it like the date of the chief's swearing in, his arrival. She had breakfast with a friend on the 12th, plenty of dinners at various neighbors' houses, notes about what she was going to bring to each dinner as part of the meal or as a gift. Her life did not seem empty or lonely.

One thing pops out more than anything else, though. Written in lime green marker but in the smallest handwriting of anything else on the board is "McManus at 11:30 p.m. ferry"; this is written under the swearing in celebration of his father. The two events happened on the same day, June 25th, which also happened to be the day she died. "Who is McManus?" Avery shouts, again hoping for the advantage of small-town knowledge.

"Your guess is as good as mine. Why?" asks Owen, coming in from the other room to see what Avery is talking about. In response, Avery merely points to the calendar, and the two exchange a look, understanding that knowing this information is a must. "That's the last ferry in for the night. Any other traffic would be monitored by the toll on the bridge, and I don't know if you know this, but it is manned at night. They have extensive knowledge of people's movement on and off this island."

"Why? What do they do with the knowledge?" Avery wonders out loud.

"Well apparently they do not solve murders. Good thing we're here. I'm going to go look in the guest bedroom," Owen says, leaving Avery to wander to the master bedroom. He feels very uncomfortable there, which is silly because she won't catch him. But it's her personal space, or at least it would be if she were still here.

The tops of the dressers are lined with picture frames. Plenty of images of Thor and Hulk stare at Avery from their frames, and he notices pictures of Officer Brown with her parents and sisters at a sister's wedding and then at her basic law enforcement training graduation. She looked really happy, her whole family did. He opened the drawers, telling himself that he wouldn't move anything, but if something were sitting out on top it is fair game. He realized after the third drawer how ridiculous he is being. If Officer Brown kept a journal, she would not have to hide it. She lived alone, so it made more sense for it to be more visible than hidden in a drawer.

Avery looks at the tables on either side of her bed, but they are pedestal tables, bare aside from matching lamps, with no storage underneath. He gets on his knees and looks under the bed, but other than forgotten dog toys, there is nothing under there. He turns toward the closet, assuming that, like his mother's, it will be filled with an endless sea of brightly colored dresses and clothes, with toppling shoe boxes and baskets for accessories. His assumption is inaccurate; police polo shirts and uniform pants are the dominant elements of the closet, hanging neatly front and center. Other than uniforms, Officer Brown didn't seem too preoccupied with clothes, so the empty space makes it easy for Avery to spot the collection of turquoise leather notebooks stacked in the corner beside her row of sandals. He pulls the first book from the top and opens it; her handwriting leaps off the page, the date on top reading May of this year.

"Guys, I found something!" he shouts. By the time his friends are in the room, Avery has pulled the stack off the floor and set them on the bed. There are six journals in all, each of them identical turquoise journals, organized chronologically, the first detailing events from three years ago.

They crowd around the bed and stare down at the books. "What's in them?" Owen asks.

Avery looks at him in disbelief. "Do you really think I read all of them in the ten minutes we have been here? I have no idea what is in these, but if there is anything to be found, any leads for us to pick up on, it has to be in here," Avery declares with confidence.

"Well, don't forget that we could find really important information on here as well," Landon motions to the laptop he carried in with him, "like recent search histories, emails she has sent or received."

Six journals, one laptop, and a name and time; hopefully, one of those things leads to some answers. "So what do we do with this stuff? Is it a good idea to take it with us?" Landon asks.

The silence lingers for a moment. To take it would be stealing, potentially stealing from a crime scene. But is it still considered a crime scene? "I say we take it with us, only for a few days. We work fast to find anything that could be helpful, and then we return it all. I don't really want to be hanging out in this house. It feels weird being here. What do you guys think?" Owen says.

"It's better we take it than someone else, right?" Avery suggests.

"But who else would be looking for it now?" Landon suggests.

"I don't know, maybe the same person who stole her boots," says Avery. Images flash through Avery's mind of the men from the security footage, the warning that they cannot trust the town council. Taking it seems like the better, safer choice.

But then Avery thinks about the trouble his dad might be in over the boots. If they get caught stealing this stuff, there's no way his dad will ever forgive him, not with that other stuff. Avery feels a wave of panic because they are already here, already made the bad decision. They just need to make the most of it.

"Okay, I've changed my mind. Maybe we stay here and read through what we can," says Avery. "If we take this stuff home, we have to break back in. We don't need to risk trouble twice, right?"

The other boys agree, perhaps because they hear the worry and panic in Avery's tone. They pop a squat right where they are. Landon opens up the laptop to see what he can do, while Owen and Avery divide the journals between them.

Avery reads through the first few pages of a journal, realizing just how much attention Officer Brown paid to everyone she came across. She would write about who she said hello to that day, people that were kind enough to pay for her coffee. There were instances of people shouting at her for trying to do her job, though. These descriptions are described in vivid detail; she must have come home and immediately wrote everything in her journal, perhaps in case she needed something for court one day. The weather, the sunrise, the color of people's shirts or hair, all of it is recorded in these books. Avery skimmed through these thoughts until he found an entry that looked a little different.

There were a few about an ex-boyfriend, but Avery had a hard time reading through these; the drama was just too much, mixed in with a bunch of Taylor Swift lyrics, the sad and angry ones.

Then he reads this: Am I always so blind to the true natures of people? If so, I will fail at being a police officer. I will believe all the wrong people, follow all the wrong leads. Maybe, then, this small beach town where they don't want me to write a single ticket is the right place for me. Maybe I will never be more than a lifeguard or babysitter with a badge.

It's hard to believe that these thoughts came from Officer Brown. She always seemed so happy and confident. But Avery recognizes these feelings of not being enough. He doesn't know how to solve this case and who to trust. He's not even sure if his friends are really his friends and if they will stick with him if he doesn't make the soccer team or when this case is over.

He shakes his head to force his focus back to the pages in front of him.

The next entry that caught Avery's attention was about the police department. It is hard to be a female in law enforcement, it is hard to be taken seriously when you are as petite as I am. But I think this problem is bigger than my size. Chief and I disagreed again about my partnering with the Carolina Beach officers. They can help teach me things about VICE that the chief won't allow me to be trained in.

This reminds Avery of what Mr. Bowen warned them about. Officer Brown thinks that Summerset has an issue with drugs, but for some reason, no one supported her. So was she wrong? Or did the last chief worry Officer Brown was too small or weak, just like Avery's dad and everyone else assumes he can't handle things because he's young. He's handled life with a VICE agent, wondering if his dad will ever make it home. He can certainly handle this investigation. Age has nothing to do with it.

He can't help but laugh at another entry. "Hey, guys, listen to this: In trouble again. A woman pulled up beside me in her golf cart today as I was getting in my car with my morning coffee in hand. She made a remark about how convenient it is for me to be getting coffee instead of getting the alligator off of the golf course. I told her that police did not deal with gators, that she would need to call animal control. She informed me that she didn't appreciate living on the same island as "that" animal, nor did she appreciate my attitude."

He closes the journal and asks, "Is that the kind of stuff you were telling me about?"

Landon doesn't take his eyes off the laptop screen, so Owen answers.

"Yeah, dude, you don't know the half of it. It's absolutely ridiculous. The tourists can have a messed up perception of reality," says Owen. "And putting up with the nonsense is all part of the job. I hear it from my dad all the time when my parents talk about their days at dinner."

Avery feels a pang of jealousy. He didn't grow up with regular family dinners. Owen's tone almost sounds bored, but Avery would love to hear about his dad's day all the time.

Owen pauses for a moment, then starts again. "I think I found something important. She wrote I think they just want me gone. I have asked repeatedly to be sent to school for VICE training, but I'm told it isn't needed. They let money rule the island. They tell me there are no drugs here, but they are lying. I have seen the transactions. I have seen low flying planes with no lights making their way silently to the island at odd hours of the night. I have seen people whose demeanors are obviously not normal.

I set up a contact at Brunswick County to work with a drug agent. He's coming to the island soon. Chief said not to trust the Brunswick County office, specifically the drug units, but that's laughable. No one should trust our drug unit. Oh wait, we don't have one, because we, of course, do not have a drug problem. Let's take a look at the numbers and types of different cases we have had this year. So many break-ins and thefts, lost children, drunk in public, and loose alligators. But how many reports about drugs? I can tell you.

Zero."

Landon looks up now. All three boys look at each other.

"Mr. Bowen was right," Landon whispers. Avery thinks he must be shocked that this is real, not just a conspiracy theory cooked up after her death.

"Yeah, and later she writes about seeing guys out in the middle of the night at the lighthouse. That must have been why she was out there the night she was killed," says Owen, his voice jarring compared to Landon's whisper.

Avery flips through a few more pages then furrows his brow. "Okay, maybe I am just wanting there to be a connection where there isn't one, but it was three guys we saw on the video, right?" He doesn't wait for an answer.

"So she wrote this entry about getting in trouble for reprimanding these three goons at the River Pilot Cafe one night. She was there alone, and they were hassling her and threatening her, so she got a little aggressive. Landon, she says that your dad was there for a while, helping her babysit them while they waited for the ferry. This happened on a Thursday. What are the odds that these three are the same ones we saw on the camera?"

"I mean, it's possible...?" Owen says. "What's happening over there with you, Landon?"

A huge smile takes over Landon's face. He turns the laptop toward his friends and begins to explain. "The password is HuThlkor@#216, which is easy enough to break but also pretty hefty." He tries to continue, but Owen is flabbergasted and interrupts.

"How could you have possibly figured that out? That's bananas!" Owen exclaims.

Landon begins to explain all the different variations he tried and why, but Owen again interrupts, "Okay, never mind, I can't even with all of this. Let's just be grateful you have the brain of a nerd and take a look."

Avery is grateful because he could kind of care less how Landon did it, he just wants to see what they can learn before they have to get out of here. And it seems they are getting a break. Thankfully, Officer Brown wasn't the type of person to close her Google Chrome down after every use. There are five tabs just waiting for examination.

Landon moves the cursor to the first tab and clicks on it. The Airbnb website stares back at them. "So everything on here basically proves what we've been saying. She didn't plan to kill herself. Owen, grab my phone and take a video of this, just in case we need it for something," says Landon.

Owen starts rolling and then Landon continues. "She was clearly planning a trip to the mountains in September. All the rentals she was looking at are in like a thirty-minute range of each other. This listing is up in Nebo. It seems just like a simple one bedroom, but let me click here... yep, she messaged the owners about bringing Thor and Hulk, explaining that they were large dogs but well-behaved and hypoallergenic."

"It was something for her to look forward to," Avery suggests. "Can you see when she started looking at these places? Or at least when she sent that message about the dogs?"

Landon squints his eyes at the screen while attempting to answer the question. "She just sent that message on the 21st. That doesn't sound like someone that isn't planning to be around," Landon said, his tone indicating that he is still thinking.

He moves the cursor to the second tab. It's for her bank account. He clicks on the sign in link, attempting a variation of her name and the same password she used for her laptop. It's rejected. He tries a different sign in name but the same password. Still denied. "Do you think I should keep trying?" Landon asks.

"I mean, I don't know much about fraud and bank accounts, but we don't know what happens when they flag an account for too many failed attempts to sign in," Owen offers.

"Yeah, and for all we know, her family has shut down the account anyway," Avery adds.

Landon turns back to the screen, quickly moving past the website for Chewy.com, and easily moving past the website where she was looking at options for hiking boots, both pretty self-explanatory. That left one more tab, the one with her email, still open. They tried to scroll through it, despite the fact that it is littered with junk mail from bookstores and event ticket vendors. There is an email about a recent purchase for tickets, for a band Avery had never heard of. "She bought two," Landon murmurs.

Avery couldn't help but wonder who the other ticket was for.

There are emails from various family members, most short and sweet and including pictures of her nieces or her sisters. Her dad kept her well updated on the state of his garden. And she kept them well updated about work, even sending a picture of the open case board that hangs in the office. "My list is the shortest!" she sent with various smiley face emojis. Landon switches tracks and looks in the trash file, though finds nothing different or unexpected there.

He moves the cursor to the sent file and scrolls through the list of emails housed there. Jumping out from the ones she has sent to her family, were the ones with professional subject lines. "She's reached out to every surrounding agency with her resume. Though it seems like she stopped towards the end of May."

"That's the same time my dad was hired," Avery adds. She did write in her journal about how she felt hope for the department knowing that he was going to be taking the helm. He flips to that page to read how she felt: The new chief is finally here, and the building just feels different, better, it just vibes on a higher energy. He isn't at all what I thought he would be. He looks young, but you can tell by the way that he handles himself that he has never let his age, whether the real number or the perception of it, get in his way. Everyone is so buttoned up, so worried about image, and yet here Fowler is with all of his tattoos. His family seems wonderful, though, each one of them authentically who they are. Even the son; his eyes are open. I feel hopeful for what this department can be.

That line about his dad's age hits him hard. If his dad isn't "too young" to be chief, Avery isn't too young to do a little digging. If anything, Officer Brown's death should teach us that life is too short.

Landon calls their attention to an email. The subject line read "Assistance needed in Summerset Island; Guaranteed Bust." The receiver is none other than Brian McManus. "Avery, that's the name from the calendar," Owen says excitedly, swinging his arm sideways and whacking Avery's arm.

The boys determined that there was nothing else for them to learn from the laptop or the journals. They put everything back to its original location.

"Did we check everything?" asks Landon.

"I only did the one spare room; did you guys hit up the other?" Owen says.

Avery and Landon both shake their heads no, and the three boys go to the door of the last room together.

Chapter 15

The door has been closed, and Avery sees now that it isn't used as a guest room at all. Part of the room is used for working out. A stationary bike is in a corner, facing a wall with a television mounted on it. Rolled up yoga mats and free weights line the wall closest to the bike, but the neighboring wall has a huge wooden desk currently covered with canvases, some completed and others not even started, of paint by number images. The desk is massive, the size of some people's dining room tables, but due to the drawers it couldn't be used for that. Birds, flowers, puppies, sunsets, and mountainscapes, all kinds of options made up the mountainous pile sitting on top of it. The desk drawers hold pots of numbered paints in bags, each labeled so she would know what painting it went with. A drop cloth is folded neatly, probably so that paint would not get on the hardwood floors. There are plastic bins filled with yarn and strings for projects Avery couldn't even begin to understand.

Owen walks to the desk and tries to yank open the center drawer, but it's locked. He tries again, with the same results: nada. "Why would she lock this drawer?" he mumbles under his breath.

Landon crawls under the desk and pulls a Swiss Army knife

out of his pocket. Avery can't see what Landon is doing, but he can hear things clicking and moving around, and the next thing he knows, the desk drawer is being pushed open from underneath the desk.

Avery peers inside, but there is nothing. "Why would you lock an empty drawer?" he asks. "And where did you learn to do that, Landon?"

Now upright, Landon shrugs and then reaches his arm inside the drawer, feeling along the top to make sure nothing is secured and hidden there. "Maybe she bought it used, and it was locked without a key. Who knows? And the Boy Scouts always tell you to be prepared."

"Yeah, I forgot that part of the motto," says Owen. "Always be ready to burglarize something."

Avery let the two of them bicker as his eyes sweep the room again. Why would this be the only door she kept closed? His eyes catch on something on the floor. Near the base of the desk, the white as faint as chalk residue, sit rainbow shaped scratches. Scratches that would have been made from someone moving the desk.

"Grab that edge and help me move this," Avery says. Both boys help Avery pull the desk away from the wall. He thinks maybe there would be a hole in the wall, a vent cover that she removed in order to hide something important, something with the answers they need to find out what happened to her.

But the wall's bare.

The back of the desk, however, has a large manila envelope taped to it.

"Oh wow! Score!" shouts Owen. Landon shushes him and gives a reminder that they are illegally in the home.

Avery reaches behind the desk and with extreme care, pulls the envelope from the back of the desk. It catches and snags, and he worries he may rip it. Through small, gentle pulls, he gets it and sets the envelope on top of the desk, not bothering to move any of the artwork that has already taken residence there. Delicately tearing it open, Avery reaches a hand inside the envelope and pulls out a thin stack of photos, blown up to be the size of your standard piece of printer paper.

The top one is of the lighthouse on Summerset Island.

"Check this. There's two guys over here, see them?" asks Owen.

"Yeah, and it looks like she didn't use the flash, probably because she was laying low," Avery says.

The first few pictures are all similar, hard to see anything worthwhile, but when Avery flips to the fourth photograph, that changes.

This picture is of a small plane, no lights, flying low over the island at night. Avery recognizes the tops of the buildings in the photo, the line of shops that create the island's main street. The next image is of the plane grounded, no one inside or around it, but it is definitely the same plane as the photograph before it. You can tell by the colors and stripes. And while it isn't the most high-quality image, it still makes out the identifying numbers, the tail numbers, on the plane that act like its license plate number.

"So, she found the drugs, right? This is what we have proof of?" Landon says, barely above a whisper.

"Holy smokes! What do we do with this? Do we take it to your dad, Avery?" asks Owen.

"No, we can't, right?" Avery asks. "Where do we say we found it? We can't tell him that we broke in. This is no good! I have no idea what to do!"

"Okay, okay, let's think. We can't tell our dads what we did because we don't want to be grounded forever. Maybe Andrew? Could we tell him?" asks Landon.

"Yeah, yeah we could probably tell Andrew. Is there any way we could find out who owns the plane? This landing strip is on the island, right?" Avery asks.

"Oh, I'm a space cadet, yes! And that kid Carter might know, right Landon? Wasn't he trying to get his pilot's license?" Owen asks. Landon nods his answer. "And there's the soccer team party tonight; he should be there. We'll go and ask him."

"I didn't really plan to go to the party tonight, but yeah, I guess we could do that. But we can't show him this picture, so I guess I'll take a picture with my cell phone?" Landon says. He takes the picture, and then Avery puts everything back in the envelope and secures it back in place behind the desk. The three of them push the desk back into its original position.

"Actually, pull it forward just a little. Just so that no one sees the marks on the floor," Avery says by way of explanation. "Let's get out of here."

They walk back through the house making sure that everything is the way they found it, turning off lights and closing doors as they had been. When they open the back door, the sunlight hits them immediately, like a police officer shining a flashlight in a perpetrator's face. That is what they are, after all. Avery begins to bend down and return the key, but he thinks better of it. Just in case someone somewhere can't be trusted, he puts the key in his pocket, and he and his two friends do their best to exit the backyard without drawing the attention of the neighbors. No curtains move, no one is on their porch. It seems today they have been successful.

Feeling safe now that they are back on the road, Avery asks about the party. He's trying not to be upset about the fact that this is the first he is hearing about it.

"Everyone calls it a soccer team party, but that's not really what it is," says Landon. "The guys on the team are there, but everyone else goes, too. Not just athletes, like, literally all the kids. So calling it a soccer party is pretty stupid."

"But it'll be good for you to go, Avery, so that you can meet people," Owen says.

Avery nods, trying to ignore that insecure feeling he has in his gut, the one that says maybe they want him to find new friends so they won't be obligated to hang out with him.

"I just can't believe what we saw today. I mean, my mind is completely blown. How did I not know this stuff was happening on the island?" asks Landon.

"I don't know if you guys realized this, but Officer Brown was not really happy at the department. According to her journals, she felt like a lot of things got overlooked and like the town wasn't really letting the officers do police work," Avery says and looks back and forth between his two friends. He is afraid that he might offend them again much like he had the day he suggested their fathers were corrupt, though he is not trying to suggest that now.

"Yeah, my dad complains about that sometimes, that they are really just on this island to babysit and for support during storms. I think my mom keeps him here. She is so afraid of what might happen to him at another department in a real city," Landon admits. "Finding Brown is without a doubt the most difficult thing he has had to deal with in his job."

"Did your dad talk to you about how everything happened? About what the crime scene looked like or what made him think he needed to leave the scene immediately?" Avery asks.

These are details his father never gave him, though he assumes that Officer Weatherby told him. Landon just shakes his head, and Avery nods. "Do you think he would talk to us about it?"

"I can ask him to," Landon says.

"Alright, so now we're pretty sure she thinks that plane has something to do with the three guys out on the lighthouse. Maybe the same three guys she arrested previously for tomfoolery," says Owen. "Do we think she knew what she was walking into at the lighthouse?"

"Maybe she was bringing backup, but instead of trusting someone here because of how many times she was shut down by the town, she went over everyone's head?" Avery is just thinking out loud here. She could have trusted his father. And that seemed really odd to him, too. "It just seems weird, though. I mean, why wouldn't she have talked to my dad. Drugs are his thing."

"Oh, really, drugs are his thing?" Owen taunts.

"Shut up, you know what I mean. He could have easily helped her. There's no way he would let these types of deals go down on the island that he had jurisdiction over," Avery says this with confidence.

Owen and Landon look at each other. "Are you sure, man? I mean, Summerset Island is not known and will never be known for its policing. The department is basically just supposed to keep things quiet and wrap everything up in a pretty bow. That is what tourists pay for, and the officers here, it's not that they like it, but they get that this is the deal. I mean, it is widely known around here that the owner of the island has told his sons that they only get possession of the island and all the money that comes with it if they can keep things looking a certain way. Maybe your dad is tired of all the high risks. Maybe he is willing to put pretty bows on everything now," Landon suggests.

Avery pictures his father, thinking back to when they were

still in New Jersey. He would come home looking exhausted, having put in crazy hours. He would sit in the middle of the night quietly and usually alone at their kitchen table eating leftovers Avery's mom would leave on the counter for him. He risked his life again and again. Maybe he is tired of that, but to give up on what he believes in… no, there is no way his dad could or would just take an easy job. If he came here, it is because he thought he could do some good here, not so that he could just coast along. Avery knows Chief Fowler believes in hard work and that sometimes risks have to be taken, not that you should just sit behind a desk and sweep things under a rug.

"No, no way. Either my dad lied to me and said he was coming to an easy, slow job, or someone lied to him."

"Well, I guess we just add that to the list of puzzles we're solving over here," says Owen.

The three boys make a plan for tonight's party, and then head their separate ways home.

***

The kitchen table is littered with delicious looking food. His mom's handmade meatballs swimming in his favorite sauce, garlic bread with melted cheese, a large bowl overflowing with spaghetti noodles, and a salad bowl filled with rainbow-colored vegetables and fruits. The meal is probably delicious, but Avery barely tastes it. He hears his parents' voices, though they sound like they are off in the distance. All he can focus on are the questions floating in his head.

Did his dad lie to him? Is someone trying to get his dad fired? Who took Officer Brown's shoes and how? Who killed her? And he can't tell if this is the most or the least important: do Landon and Owen like him, or are they stuck with him?

He takes another bite of meatball, chewing it slowly. "What's up with you, kid?" demands his mother, the tone in her voice forcing him to attention. "This is your favorite meal. Why are you acting like it is torture to have to eat it?" His mom sounds irritated, but her eyes are soft and open, her mouth slightly smiling to show concern. As usual, his father cleared his plate; he is a big stickler for not wasting food. Avery looks at his own plate and realizes how little he has actually eaten. He scoops another mound of spaghetti onto his fork and shoves it into his mouth.

"When I saw Andrew today, he said your lesson went well," says Chief Fowler before taking another bite of salad.

"You saw Andrew today?" Avery asks, now worried that Andrew might mention how much time the boys have been spending there and exactly what they have been doing.

"I had to go by there for work," his dad says. "The hardware store had a break-in, and I asked Andrew if he had noticed anything suspicious and just told him to be a little more aware."

"They send the chief of police to deal with break-ins?" Avery asks. In New Jersey, his dad's department was huge. He had a specific job and role. His dad explains that here, in such a small department, people need to be willing to roll up their sleeves and do whatever is needed of them.

"From what I understand, the detectives have a good bit of experience with home burglaries, but this is new for them," says the chief. "Still, the procedures would be the same, and they're coming up with nothing. Either these were highly intelligent and professional criminals, or there was no break-in. It's very... odd. But we'll get it figured out."

Avery wants to ask about whether or not his dad is still looking into Officer Brown's case, but he knows better to bring that up and bring attention to himself. He clears his plate and asks to be excused to walk the dogs. He's granted permission, slides from his chair and follows the dogs to the hooks where their leashes hang. The sooner he gets this over with, the sooner he can get to the party and, hopefully, some answers.

When he gets back, his parents have already finished with the dishes and are relaxing on the porch swing, his mom's legs tucked underneath her and his dad lackadaisically rocking the bench, each with a book in their hands. He wishes he could sit out there and enjoy the night with them, but there's work to be done.

"If it's alright with you guys, I'm gonna meet up with Landon and Owen and go to this soccer team party."

His dad doesn't even look up from his page. "Are you sure that's a good idea? Don't you have your soccer tryout tomorrow?"

Oh, yeah, that. "I practiced a little before dinner, and I should have time in the morning to practice some more. We won't be late. I just want to meet some of the other guys," says Avery.

It looked like his dad was about to say something, but Avery's mom jumps in. "As you should. You can go for a few hours, but you leave us the address and your father will be there at 10. And that's a summer curfew, by the way. Don't get used to it."

"Ummm, seriously? Dad has to pick me up?"

"Yeah, do I have to do that?" his dad asks.

"Oh, seriously, the two of you are trying to kill me. Yes, that's how it's going down. Take it or leave it, kid," she says, giving Avery's dad the side eye.

He takes it.

He goes into his room to change his shirt, changes it again. Looking in the mirror, he wonders what everyone else will be wearing. But a clean t-shirt from a local surf shop and pair of shorts can't make it look like he's trying too hard, right? He hopes not as he puts on his flip flops.

***

The three boys walk down the street, Avery still marveling that they can walk right down the center and not a single car could get in their way. Each of the homes that they pass seem quiet, like the people inside are done for the day and the house is tucking them in. No one sits on their front porch, but Avery thinks that's probably because they would prefer to be on the back porches to see the ocean and get a better breeze. It feels very quiet and safe.

Owen is telling Avery about the house they are going to. It is apparently one of the biggest on the island, and the kid whose parents own it is on the team, but not because of his soccer abilities.

"Just another example of how money can set you apart around here," Owen says.

The house towers in front of them. It looks like it is made of glass, some plain and see-through, other sections frosted and white. Its height is impossible to ignore, and the lawn is filled with palm trees and cacti making it look like a cross between a beach and a desert. Owen knocks on the door, and moments later it swings in. The noise level is high from music pumping through speakers mounted in the corners of each room and, of course, all the chatter. It looks like pretty close to one hundred kids are here.

"Before we forget, let's wander around and try to find Carter," says Landon.

Avery notices Owen fist bumping and high fiving people as he goes past and wishes that he were as comfortable and confident right about now. He sees a group of guys surrounding a large air hockey table, each of them in a polo shirt of a different color. They looked like a collection of Easter eggs, though these would be Easter eggs that also wear puka shell necklaces. He wonders if this is their version of a BFF necklace. Weird.

There's a huge television mounted to a nearby wall, and mounds of kids are playing FIFA or cheering for those playing. The kids currently with controllers in their hands stare intently at the screen, like a real trophy is on the line. Plenty in this huddle have jerseys on, some with the Hammerheads logo, but others with Manchester United or Chelsea or Real Madrid. These guys are probably on the soccer team, Avery assumes. He wishes he could introduce himself to a few people, but Landon seems to be on a mission to find that Carter kid.

They pass the area that has a ton of snacks and head out to the pool. Past the splashing and laughing, the bright colors of trunks and bikinis, and the bouncing beach balls, Avery sees where Landon is headed: over to a corner where a kid is lying in the small patch of grass staring at the sky.

Carter is wearing well-laundered jeans and a button-up shirt. He seems more finely polished than most at this party. Avery wonders if his mom picks out his clothes.

"Hey, Carter, how's it going?" asks Landon, loud enough to be heard over all the background noise.

Carter tilts his head backwards to see who is speaking to him, then he smiles in greeting. Landon introduces Avery to Carter, and they say what's up before Landon gets to business.

"How's everything going with your pilot's license?" he asks.

Carter sits up now to talk to the group. "It's lame, but I have to be sixteen to get the actual license. Until then, I get to keep practicing with whoever is willing to let me into their plane. I've logged an obscene number of hours already."

"Good for you, man. That's awesome. What got you into planes?" asks Avery, just making casual conversation.

"My parents used to joke that you couldn't keep me out of them. My dad is a commercial pilot. Some people fish with their dad, others play ball, I fly," Carter says.

Avery and his father don't really have a thing, but hopefully they will if they get to stay in Summerset Island. After today, that seems like a big if.

"Cool, cool," begins Owen. "Listen, man, we have a random question for you. Would you recognize a tail number from one of the planes if we ran it by you?"

Carter furrows his brow. Yeah, it's a random question all right. "Um, maybe? I guess it would depend on the number and how often it's around the air strip."

Landon spouts out the number from memory. Carter sits quietly for a minute, obviously scanning his memory for that number. Avery and his friends exchange a look, and Avery finds himself getting impatient. He realizes how desperate they are for Carter to know the right answer because otherwise, this is just another dead end.

"I could be wrong, but I am pretty sure that sequence is on the plane that Mr. Ramsey owns. Though he's not the only one who flies it. I think he lets some other guys on the town council use it. But I've also seen some random people flying it. Maybe he rents it out? IDK. I could double check next time I'm out there."

"Mr. Ramsey? The hardware store Mr. Ramsey? What would he need a plane for?" asks Owen, seemingly reading Avery's mind.

"Yeah, I don't think it's like a need thing, as much as just a hobby," Carter says. "Unless maybe he gets certain supplies for his store that way. I guess that's possible. I've never paid that much attention."

"Well, thanks, Carter. That was really helpful," says Landon.

"For sure, but why do you ask?"

Uh oh, Avery didn't think about a reason to give for their question. Landon's eyes grow wide, clearly not prepared to fumble through a story either, and Avery doesn't know this kid well enough to know whether he needs to lie or just shoot him straight.

Owen saves them, though. "Check this, we were out at Avery's house the other night, playing soccer on the beach, and we saw this plane coming in pretty low. It kinda creeped us out. Landon snapped a picture of it, and we thought if anyone would know who was flying that thing, it would be you."

"Were his lights on or off?" asks Carter. "Because I see his plane out a lot without his lights, and I wonder if something is wrong with his plane. Why would you be flying without your lights on?"

"You see his plane out without lights on a lot? Is it really late at night?" Avery asks.

"Yeah, I sit outside a lot of nights doing just what you caught me doing here tonight. I prefer the sky to most people, no offense. You guys are cool, but some of these guys are too extra for me. I've fallen asleep a few times in the back yard and woken up to the sounds of the plane."

So here's a living, breathing person that can account for seeing the plane out late at night, no lights, flying low! This is a witness! They have found a witness, thinks Avery.

"Carter, can you get in trouble for flying without your lights on?" asks Avery.

"Yeah, they are supposed to keep track of that at the air strip, but since it's a private strip and people aren't working 24/7, he probably gets a free pass," Carter says.

Avery transitions the conversation to something completely different so that Carter feels like they care about more than just interrogating him. Avery asks if he's in eighth grade, too, and whether he's on the soccer team.

"We'll probably have a few classes together," says Carter, "but you won't see me on the soccer field. Soccer's not really my thing. But if you go out for Student Government, you will see me there."

"That sounds cool. Maybe I'll look into it," says Avery.

"Alright, well our curfew is quickly approaching, and we want to make sure Avery meets a few other people before school starts. Thanks again, Carter," says Landon.

They turn around and walk back towards the house, Owen mumbling about how he would like to be introduced to some food.

"Dude, how are you always so hungry?" Landon asks.

Avery is laughing, scanning the crowd for faces he may have seen around town. And then he sees something. He stops immediately, causing Owen to bump into him.

"Hey, Avery, where'd you learn to walk because here in North Carolina we tend to put one foot in front of the other!" says Owen.

Avery doesn't respond, though. He just points in the direction of a group of girls. It isn't because of what they are doing or how they look, but because of what one of them is wearing...on her feet.

Landon sees what Avery is pointing at first.

"Are those what I think they are?" Landon asks.

"I mean, they have to be, right? No one else has boots like those. Cops and military, that's it," says Avery. "We've got to ask her about them."

"Yeah, about that. She won't tell me or Landon jack squat," Owen says. "That's Delaney Keller. She's in eighth grade with us, but her boyfriend is in high school. Don't ask me how that works or why. She knows us, knows who our dads are. But she doesn't know you, so if we have any hope in getting an answer, it's going to be from you. Maybe just don't say your last name. Or your first. Say as little as possible."

"Yeah, okay, maybe I can just point to her feet, grunt, and shrug," Avery says, his voice thick with sarcasm.

"Sure, whatever floats your boat, man, just get in there. Landon, get your phone and record this," says Owen.

Avery makes his way over to the group of girls, none of them dressed in the summery, bright colors that a lot of the other girls are flaunting. Some have band t-shirts on, maybe that they have bought from Andrew, but probably not. Avery would have seen them around the shop by now. Delaney is the center of attention, and Avery can hear her talking to her audience. She's very loud, and her tone has no lightness, no laughter in it. She's not really smiling as much as snarling. If Avery had to describe her in a word, it'd be salty.

"Those are some pretty serious boots," he says, walking up beside her.

Delaney turns her attention to Avery, looking him up and down with... disgust? Suspicion? Her eyes are kind of squinted, and there is still no smile.

"Yeah, they're great for stomping on unwanted things and people," she says, and the girls behind her laugh and snicker at her response and Avery's wide eyes.

"Oh, wow. That's not the answer I expected. Where can someone get a pair of boots like that?" asks Avery, trying to keep his voice steady. He's never met a girl, or any human really, as unfriendly as Delaney Keller. He's not ready for her bite.

"Really? You want to know where to buy boots? That's why you're over here?" Delaney says through her laughter. "You know what, you're really lame. You should get out of here before my boyfriend gets here."

"Sorry, I wasn't trying to..." he pauses, "I didn't know you had a boyfriend. Did he get you the boots?"

She rolls her eyes and seems to be done with Avery and the whole conversation. Avery's weak smile is fading; he's struck out.

Then a girl in the circle smiles at him, a real smile, one that actually hits her eyes. "Yeah, he sure did. Some girls like flowers, but Delaney over here wants stolen boots. I'd be happy if someone cared enough to bring me a soda."

And BOOM, he's back in the game. "What kind?" he asks.

She smiles again and says to surprise her. Avery turns and walks to the doors. He steps inside and pushes his way past the kids crowded around the counter towards the fancy buckets filled with ice and drinks. He reaches in and grabs two sodas then jostles his way back out the doors and to the girl.

She takes a few steps away from her crowd; Avery holds the drinks out to her, telling her to pick her poison. She smiles and grabs the Dr. Pepper.

"What's your name?" he asks.

"I'm Marissa. Don't mind D. She's intense, but she thinks she has to be in order to impress her boyfriend who's, like, super old."

"And he stole boots for her? That's kind of random," says Avery.

"Oh, it's definitely random," Marissa says. "But he thinks he's super cool. He said someone paid him to steal them, so he got a gift for his girl and some cash. He seems like a creep, but whatevs. What's your name, anyway?"

"Oh, sorry. I'm Avery. My family and I just moved here, and some kids invited me to the party when I went into school to sign up for a soccer tryout."

He sticks his hand out to shake hers, but she just squints her eyes and smirks at him. Note to self, girls don't want to shake your hand apparently.

"I guess I'll see you around this year, Avery," she says. "Thanks for the soda."

Avery smiles and offers an awkward little wave before wandering off. What in the world was that, he asks himself. He's happy to escape into a sea of strangers and try to pretend he didn't just experience that moment.

"Dude, what in the world was that?" Owen asks. "Even Landon is smoother!"

"You're not wrong, man. That was bad, so bad. But hey, she said that Delaney's boyfriend heisted the boots, and that he was paid to do it," says Avery. "Landon, were you able to get a clear image of them? My dad should be here soon."

"Yep, we got it!"

Chapter 16

By 9:50 the boys are already waiting at the end of the driveway for Chief Fowler to pull up in his truck. Owen has asked what time it is so many times Avery is ready to pull his hair out, and now he bounces on his toes staring longingly down the road looking for headlights he recognizes.

"Oh, finally, here he comes!" Avery says, throwing his arms up in relief and smiling wide. When his dad comes to a stop in front of them, Avery yanks the door open to the passenger side. "Dad, I don't think I have ever been so happy to see you. We have to tell you something!"

"Sweet. It's not every day people are actually happy to get into my car," jokes the chief. "Hop in, fellas."

The three boys clamor in and pull the doors closed behind them. Chief Fowler begins to drive back the way he came, and Landon, Owen, and Avery all try to talk at once. Avery can barely hear himself think, and he knows his father can't possibly understand a word.

The chief slams on breaks, sending the three boys flying forward in their seats in a jerking motion. "How about we try one at a time?" he says.

"We found the boots!" Owen shouts.

"Yeah, I need more information," says the chief.

"Dad, there's a girl inside bragging about how her boyfriend stole her a pair of police boots. And he got paid to do it," says Avery. "She said all of it, we got it on camera, though I don't know how clearly you can hear it, but we are your witnesses, forget the camera."

"Okay, let me see what you're talking about. Whose boots exactly do you think she's wearing?" Chief Fowler asks.

Landon passes his phone, the video already on the screen, up to the chief.

"Officer Brown's boots, Dad. That's whose boots," Avery says.

"Yes, but how did you know that the boots went missing, Avery?" asks his dad. "That information was not disclosed to anyone outside of the department."

Owen begins whistling nonchalantly in the backseat. Chief Fowler looks pointedly at him, his lips in a straight line, and he waits.

Realizing that the chief will not be moving on from the topic or diverting his attention any time soon, Owen speaks up. "Well, you see, what had happened was that Maggie had those pictures on her desk. And it didn't take a genius to see that in one image there were boots and in another image, there were no boots."

"So, let me get this straight, while Avery was in my office asking me about the missing evidence, you helped yourself to information on Maggie's desk?" Chief Fowler asks, his tone serious and sharp, impatience lingering on the edges, too.

"Well, it was just sitting out. It's not like she said it was a secret or tried to cover it up," says Owen.

Chief Fowler runs his hands down his face and exhales. "Of course, she wouldn't have. You're a kid, and a cop's kid at that. She figured you couldn't be less interested." He watches the video, his eyes going wide in recognition of the boots when they appear on the screen. It's hard to hear everything, but enough is audible to be usable. The chief airdrops the video from Landon's phone to his then dials a number.

"Hey, how fast can you get here?" he says into the phone. A few grunts and mumbled statements follow, it's like some kind of weird code Avery can't follow.

"This is so cool! Did you just call for backup?" asks Owen.

"No, I got you kids a ride. Your work here is done. Seriously, good observational skills. You saved us a lot of time, but I can't have you around for what happens next. I'm going to step out and make a phone call."

And he does, loudly closing the car door behind him.

"Are you kidding me? We did all that and we didn't even get a high five or a head nod or anything. Just a good looking out now get out of the car?" Owen says.

Avery is frustrated, too. He expected his dad to be a lot more excited about this information and to be proud of them, not to seem irritated that they knew what to be looking for. If he's acting this way about the boots, imagine how he would act if he knew the boys had broken into Officer Brown's house. It's really discouraging. It's also kind of annoying that his dad won't even let them listen in to his phone call. And they are going to be carted off without even getting to see Delaney escorted out of the party.

Avery can see headlights coming in their direction. Jeep headlights to be specific. His mom. "This is not the kind of backup I had in mind," Avery mutters.

Owen, Landon, and Avery climb down from the truck. Chief Fowler ends his call and looks at the three, each wearing frowns.

"We can help, though, Chief," says Landon. "Like, we can find out who Delaney's boyfriend is."

"Thanks for the offer, Landon, but Instagram and SnapChat already took care of that. Let this be a lesson to stay off social media of you want to make sure you never get caught doing something stupid. Better, just don't be stupid," says Chief Fowler. "Seriously, thank you for bringing this information to me. Avery, we're going to have a chat when I get home."

Avery's eyes go wide, panic written on his face. A chat about what, he thinks to himself. But he can't ask because his dad's phone starts ringing, and as Avery has long since learned, his dad will always answer the call when it's work.

He climbs into the front seat of his mom's Jeep, Landon and Owen scrambling into the back.

"So, how was the party? Tell me all about it," says Avery's mom.

"Avery flirted with a girl," Owen shouts from the back seat, and then he and Landon burst into a fit of giggles.

It was what Avery needed, something to release the tension and distract from how bummed out he is that his dad basically dismissed them like useless children. He laughed, too, especially when he saw the side eye his mom gave him.

"Who's the girl, huh? Will I like her?" she asks.

"Oh, no, Mrs. Fowler, this girl is nothing but trouble," says Landon. "Avery didn't really want to talk to her, but we kind of needed him to so we could figure a few things out."

"Ahh, trouble. Yes, I know it well. Be careful, kiddo. And also, let's not make a habit of using people just to get information from them. That hurts people's feelings. That goes for all of you."

A round of yes ma'ams went through the Jeep. "Well, is trouble at least pretty? Seriously, tell me the stories!" says Mrs. Fowler.

No longer chastened, they laugh, and Landon and Owen take turns letting her know about the party, who was there, and that Avery will be just fine.

***

Back at home, Avery flops down on his bed, glad to have the comfort of Thor and Hulk around him. He stares at the ceiling and wonders what his dad is going to say to him. How worried should he really be right now?

"Knock knock," says his mom, coming into the room to pet the dogs for a moment and kiss the top of Avery's head. "Goodnight, my bear."

"Mom, when am I going to be too old for you to call me Avery bear?" he asks with a serious look on his face.

"Just be glad I don't call you that in front of your friends." She stops petting the dogs and looks into her son's face. "What's up, kid? How are you?"

Terrible. Terrified. Stressed out. "I'm fine, mom," Avery says.

"Really? Is this the face of fine these days? Because it's pretty terrifying."

"I'm not on drugs," he says, not really knowing why.

She squints her eyes at him and laughs. "Well, I didn't think that you were until this moment. But I would hope that you would realize that with your father, there is no way you would get away with doing drugs. He would know. And then he might kill you, all things considered." She smiles and tilts her head a little to the side. "I know it is not drugs, Avery, but something is up with you. You look exhausted. Can I help? Is it soccer related or about Officer Brown or about making friends?"

He exhales loudly. "Can it be all of the above?"

"Of course, it can be, bear. You've gone through a lot recently. A lot of change and then something very traumatic. It is completely okay not to be okay. But you have to talk to me," she says.

"Honestly, right now I am just worried that I'm somehow in trouble with Dad."

"Well, did you do what he asked you not to do?" she asks.

Avery hates lying to his mom, but he also knows she won't keep anything from his dad, so he's got to keep this secret for as long as he can. Besides, he didn't really hurt anything. They talked to Mr. Bowen, no big deal. They searched the video footage, but Andrew allowed that, and it's his footage, so whatever. Yes, they snooped and found out about the doctor's name and his diagnosis for Officer Brown, and yes, they kinda broke into her house. But they have nothing but good intentions.

Seriously, nothing. No real answers, just good intentions.

So he lies. "No, mom, we haven't done anything. It was a total coincidence that we bumped into this girl tonight."

"Well, then there is nothing to be worried about. Get to sleep. You have a big day tomorrow. I love you," Mrs. Fowler says, hitting the light switch on her way to the door.

"Love you, too, Mom." She smiles back at him and closes the door softly.

Chapter 17

Avery barely sleeps all night. Maybe it's stress about his dad wanting to talk to him, maybe it's nerves about soccer tryouts, or maybe it's about someone stealing evidence. Because if someone is willing to pay to have that evidence stolen, there is a reason. Avery just wishes he knew what it was.

What he does feel confident in is that he doesn't like the idea of those photos from Officer Brown's house being left behind in the house. This case clearly isn't over, and that is sensitive, important information.

He wishes he could solve that dilemma now, but he can't be late for soccer tryouts. So much is riding on these tryouts: his friendships, his confidence, and the moments of seeing his dad cheer for him. Yeah, no big deal at all.

Avery pulls on his shorts and agonizes over whether he should wear his Hammerheads jersey. Is it good luck, or is it jinxing himself? He can't risk it, so a plain t-shirt it is. He swings his door open and allows Thor and Hulk to bound down the hallway toward the kitchen. Avery isn't expecting to see his dad sitting at the kitchen table. He's usually long since at work by now.

"Where's Mom?" Avery asks, hoping that if she's here his dad won't bring up whatever he wants to talk about.

"She's out on the beach taking a yoga class."

"Umm, didn't you guys used to make fun of people who did that?" asks Avery.

The chief smiles while taking a sip of his coffee. "Yeah, but now we need to fit in with the locals or whatever."

After dumping cups of food into the dogs' bowls, Avery opens the refrigerator and grabs a bowl with yogurt, blackberries, and almond slices. He also claims the bagel with peanut butter left for him on the counter. He sits down at the table and tears into his breakfast, shoveling yogurt into his mouth then hastily biting into the bagel.

"Really? Are you that ravenous? We fed you dinner last night," Chief Fowler says.

"I know, but I have tryouts and the other day Owen ate my breakfast because it was unattended, and we didn't have the door locked. I guess I am still hungry from that."

"We always lock the door, though," says his dad.

"Well, not that morning."

His dad asks him to remember specifically what morning it was, but Avery can hardly remember what he ate for lunch yesterday. His mind is cluttered with too much other stuff.

"Fair enough," says Chief Fowler before getting down to business. "Look, I'm not trying to stress you out on the morning of your tryout, but I need to know. Did you guys come to the station the other day to find out what was stolen? Were you doing exactly what I asked you not to do?"

Avery puts down the spoon and swallows hard. His heart is racing; his dad is a smart man and good at his job. How much does he already know? He's never really lied to his dad, mostly because his dad wasn't around much. Does he want to start now?

Maybe he just tells his dad a little bit.

"No. We saw the news vans and got nosy, but when I went into your office, I had no idea Owen was out there snooping around Maggie's desk," says Avery. "And that wasn't our plan when we came over to the station. I know you were upset after we pulled the stunt to get into the conference room, so I wouldn't do that again."

His dad's gray-blue eyes search his face. "And?"

How does he know there's an and, Avery thinks.

"And we did look through the video footage at Andrew's store. Landon found images of two guys and a partial of their license plate."

Chief Fowler smiles at that. "And what were you going to do with that information?"

Avery runs both hands through his hair, exasperated. "Clearly nothing! Our only option would be to look in every garage on the island, but we realized that you had the video, so we wasted our time."

"Avery, I love that you are so committed to this, and that you want to help out and be involved. Officer Brown would be honored that you care this much," he says as he reaches out to put his hand on Avery's shoulder. "But she would also want you to kick some butt in your tryout today and just be thirteen. This is dangerous, bud. It's not a game."

"I'm not stupid, Dad," Avery says with his voice raised. "I know it's dangerous. But we're being careful."

He's tired of being talked down to like he's oblivious or dumb.

"No, you're not being anything," says his dad. "I don't know why I need to say this again, Avery. Stay. Out. Of. This. I am trying to protect you. Don't make me take soccer away. But if you can't respect what I am saying to you, that's where this is headed."

"Dad! That's not fair! I am just trying to help," Avery pleads, but his father interrupts.

"You have been asked repeatedly not to help. And life isn't fair, Avery. Do you think Officer Brown thinks that what happened to her was fair? The sooner you accept this reality, the easier life becomes, man. Do you understand the expectation?"

"Yes, I do." Avery stands from the table and brings his dishes to the dishwasher. He grabs his water bottle and fills it at the refrigerator.

"Don't worry about walking the dogs this morning. I've got them. Good luck at your tryout," says Chief Fowler. Avery tries to understand the expression on his dad's face. He knows his dad doesn't like being the bad guy at home; he does it enough at work. So this, not being involved, must be important to him. But finding the truth for Officer Brown and protecting his dad is important to Avery.

Besides, right now, he doesn't want to take it easy on his dad.

So instead of saying thank you and asking his dad to come with him, he mumbles a thanks and heads out the door.

Yeah, thanks a lot for messing with my head space right before a tryout, thinks Avery. Seriously, he couldn't have waited until after the tryouts?

Avery rides his bike to the school alone, waving to people as he goes, noticing the flashy cars in some of the driveways and the pristine landscaping in others. He's breathing deeply, not because of the exertion from the bike but to distract himself from his nerves. What will it mean if he doesn't make the team? It's easy to envision life on the island if he has a spot on the team, but if he doesn't, Avery has no clue how he's going to find a place in school. Or how he will show his dad that he is actually good at something.

There's a lone Durango in the parking lot by the soccer fields, and Avery assumes that it must belong to Coach Gilmore. The green grass is shining in the morning sun, still wet with dew. It's a beautiful sight. He leaves his bike by the sidewalk and jogs over to where the coach is adjusting one of the goals.

"Good morning, Coach Gilmore," Avery says, hoping he sounds more confident than he feels.

"Hey, Avery. Good to see you. Are you ready for today?"

Avery just nods in response, afraid that if he speaks too much, he will make a fool of himself, he's that nervous.

"Okay, normally we would have a large group of boys out here to help us with this," says Coach Gilmore, "and it usually goes on for a few days, but today it will be just you and me. I'm still going to want to see your speed, endurance, agility, and accuracy, but it will be in bite-sized demonstrations. Let's get started. Get to the line and run at top speed to the goal and back. I'm timing you, so on my mark."

Coach blows the whistle and Avery takes off at top speed, keeping his feet as light as possible, feeling every muscle in his legs contract and expand to propel him forward. He can't remember a time when he has ever run this fast. He makes it to the goal and turns, pumping his arms and keeping his eyes on the coach, specifically the stopwatch in his hand. One foot in front of the other, again and again until he is to the other side of the field.

He hears the beep of the stopwatch as he crosses the line.

"That's a great time, Avery. Good job," says Coach Gilmore.

Avery's relieved he started strong. Coach explains the next maneuver, a simple drill to see his accuracy into the goal undefended, and Avery again does well, managing to get five of seven into the goal, despite the angles and distance of some of the balls.

He chugs some water before his next task is explained to him.

"Okay, we're going to go one on one here," Coach Gilmore says. "You'll be on defense first, then we'll switch after a few minutes and you will try to score on me. Just do your best to knock the ball away from me."

"Got it," says Avery, and the coach smiles in return. Avery's dripping with sweat, both from the heat and his nerves, but it's getting a little better as he goes. Coach Gilmore dribbles down the field, and Avery stays light on his toes, watching for a pattern in the coach's stride or dribble. He thinks he has it figured out, and he advances toward the coach, his foot crashing into the ball and sending it flying across the field. He smiles wide, excited and proud. Coach whistles and nods in response.

"Nice! Keep that up. Let's try it again," he says before running after the ball and making his way toward the goal again.

Like a cat after a mouse, Avery pounces again. They go through the drill ten times before reversing roles. The coach only got past him twice, and Avery feels like that's a pretty decent performance.

They switch sides, Coach Gilmore now standing in Avery's way, towering over him, and it's as if a switch in Avery's brain just flips. He can't get it together. He attempts to weave past the coach, and he trips on his own feet. All Avery can see is his dad standing in his way, and he shakes his head trying to recover.

It doesn't work. Each time they reset the drill, Avery stumbles again, turning the ball over. He can't make it anywhere near the goal.

"Why don't you take a quick break while I set up for the agility drill. You're doing great, Avery. Just get your focus back," says the coach.

"Thanks, Coach. Sorry, I don't know what happened out there," Avery says before going to get some water and hopefully clear his head.

He bounces a little bit on the sidelines, waiting for the drill to be set up and yelling at himself for being distracted. Who cares that his dad is mad at him and thinks he's too big of a baby to help in Officer Brown's investigation? He doesn't need his dad's approval.

Except he does. He wants it, so badly.

Coach Gilmore calls him over and explains how to maneuver around the series of cones before shooting into the goal. It's an elaborate path, but nothing impossible.

At least not if you have the ability to concentrate. Avery squeezes his eyes closed for a few moments before letting the side of his foot tap the ball to begin. It wasn't a tap, though. He kicks it too hard and has to recover, then he misses a cone completely, and knocks the next one over. It's a mess. He keeps going, though, and aims for the goal, barely making it despite the fact that it's empty of a defender.

Avery shakes his head, completely disgusted with himself. He should have practiced more. His dad was right; he was lazy and not well prepared. He covers his eyes for a minute with both hands before running them through his hair in frustration. He knows the coach is watching his every move.

"I'm sorry, Coach. Can I try it again?" asks Avery.

The coach walks over to where Avery stands in front of the goal. He places a hand on Avery's shoulder. Panic fills Avery. This is where he learns he won't be playing soccer this year.

"You know what? I think we'll try again another day. You came out the gate swinging, but I think you psyched yourself out.

Go home, clear your head. Can you meet at the same time tomorrow?" Coach Gilmore asks.

"Yes, sir," says Avery. "Can I help you clean up?"

"That's nice of you to offer, but really, go rest up. Tomorrow will be better."

Avery puts his backpack on, walks to his bike, and takes off in the direction of Landon's house. He is flooded with so many emotions. He's frustrated with himself, but also with his dad for messing with his head this morning. He's grateful for an extra day but also terrified that he will make an even bigger fool of himself tomorrow. And he is embarrassed. It's almost better to avoid Landon and Owen until tomorrow than have to tell them the truth. But he pedals on anyway.

***

"Lemme make sure I get this. Basically, based upon the fact that Delaney's creepy old man boyfriend was paid to steal Officer Brown's boots, you think someone is out to either make your dad or the entire police department look bad," says Landon. "And you are connecting this to the burglary at Mr. Ramsey's hardware store?"

"Yeah, did your dad say anything to you about it?"

Avery is in Landon's room, sprawled out in a huge bean bag chair. Landon is sitting in his desk chair; he was working on some code for a new computer game when Avery arrived. Avery apologized for interrupting, but Landon had said he was happy for the company.

"He mentioned something the other night at dinner, though I wasn't really listening. He teased my mom about not being able to go there for a few days because, you know, she's always working on something around here," says Landon. He pauses for a minute to think. "Oh, I know. He said something about how convenient it was that the night the store was broken into was the same day the store's security system malfunctioned."

"Really? Your dad told you that?" asks Avery, a little hurt that his dad didn't share that information with him. He imagines that Landon and his dad spend a decent amount of time together, and he feels a pang of jealousy.

"Well, told my mom, really. By that point I was leaving the room. It's like they think I can't hear them sometimes. Hello, I am still in the room! Ya know?"

Avery knows exactly what Landon means.

"Alright, so the evidence room gets broken into, here's this burglary they haven't solved yet, and they weren't allowed to assist on the murder of Officer Brown because they are inexperienced," says Avery. "The department is not looking good. So maybe we send those pictures to them, like, anonymously, of the plane. The return address could be Officer Brown's address, and someone would connect the dots, right?"

Landon hesitates to answer, but then nods, picks up his phone, and calls Owen.

Chapter 18

"How'd the tryout go, bro?" asks Owen.

The three boys are walking to Officer Brown's house, sticking to sidewalks in order to not stick out so much. Instead of his normal booming tone, Owen's voice is a little lower today. They're all in stealth mode.

"Oh, I totally forgot to ask. I just assumed it was good. Sorry, Avery," says Landon.

Avery shrugs and tells them what happened, beginning with his dad getting on his case that morning and ending with him choking.

"Man, that's brutal. No worries, you'll get it tomorrow," says Owen.

"I hope so. I don't know who I will hang out with if I'm not on the team," admits Avery. He keeps his head down after saying this, a little embarrassed that he's shared this thought at all.

Owen elbows him a little.

"What are you talking about?" Owen asks. "Why wouldn't you still hangout with us?" His brows are furrowed in confusion, and he isn't smiling.

"Well, I just figured that if I wasn't on the team with you..." Avery says, but trails off. His cheeks are red in embarrassment.

"Avery, we'll still be friends even if you don't make the team," Landon says, his voice much more patient than Owen's. Landon is squinting into the sun, and Avery thinks he must realize what Avery's been so concerned about. Landon's like that, more quiet, more analytical.

"Obviously we'll still be friends!" says Owen, exasperation filling his voice. "Seriously, we're solving all the world's problems together, I mean. Really."

The three laugh together at that, and even though Avery knows they are about to do something that could get him into a lot of trouble with his dad, he feels a lot better.

They arrive in front of Officer Brown's house, the key tucked safely in Avery's pocket.

Everything looked the same as it had out front yesterday afternoon. The boys walk to the gate and push it open, glad that this time they will not have to inspect each flowerpot. As they walk, single file, through the back yard, Landon suggests that after they get the photos into the mail slot in the middle of town, they head to Avery's to practice for his second tryout.

Avery takes a step through the door, but only a single step. Owen and Landon are stuck outside, their view of the house obscured by Avery.

"Hey, Avery, you have to actually walk in the house so that we can get in too," Landon says.

Owen laughs and adds, "Look at Landon actually cracking jokes today."

Avery turns around, and the look on his face stops their laughter immediately. Avery's face has turned white, and his eyes are wide.

"Someone's been here, you guys. And they were looking for something," he says.

Avery turns back toward the house and steps further inside, carefully finding a place to land his steps because the entryway is filled with shards of broken glass. Landon closes the door behind himself, and the three boys survey what they can see from where they are standing.

The window next to the door is broken, causing all of the pieces of shattered glass they are currently stepping on. Whoever broke it must have then reached in the window to unlock the door. Kitchen cabinets are open haphazardly, drawers have been flung open, one looking close to completely falling out at any moment. What had once been organized is now in complete disarray.

The trail of destruction continues on into the living room, where books that had been on a shelf are now dumped onto the floor, some of them laying open as if whoever did this thought something important could be hidden inside one of them. The cushions on the couch are slashed open, their contents overflowing, spewing out from the fabric that once contained it. The framed artwork that had been carefully and strategically hung on the wall is ripped from it, its backing torn off. The desk drawers, like those in the kitchen, were taken from their homes, contents dumped on the floor.

The house has been destroyed. And this ransacking happened less than twenty-four hours ago.

Without saying a word, Landon reaches into his pocket and pulls out his phone. He taps Avery's arm to get his attention and holds the phone out to him. Avery immediately dials his dad's number and tells him where they are and what has happened. The call takes less than thirty seconds.

"He'll be here in a second," says Avery, handing Landon back his phone.

"What are you going to do, man?" asks Landon. "Your dad told you not to mess with this investigation."

"What if we say we were getting something for the dogs?" Owen asks.

"Like what? What do they need that requires us breaking in here?" asks Landon. A challenge is in his voice because lying to your cop fathers doesn't always go well.

There's a silence that settles over them. Avery racks his brain for anything that might help.

Owen snaps his fingers.

"I really amaze myself sometimes! You didn't bring their anxiety vests to your house, did you, Avery?"

Avery shakes his head in response, still confused as to where this is going.

Owen smiles wide. "I didn't think so. The fourth of July is this week, and Thor and Hulk freak out during fireworks. They need their vests, and we're here to get them," he says. "Boom!"

Avery smiles at him, relief flooding him. Boom indeed. That story could work. He feels guilty because he knows he shouldn't lie to his dad, but he also wants to play soccer.

The sound of gravel crunching can be heard. Their cover story was cooked up just in time.

Chief Fowler and Lt. Weatherby arrive, carefully pushing open the back door. The boys haven't moved since they arrived, too afraid to disturb any evidence.

"Explain to me why you are here," the chief says. It's a demand. There is no light in his eyes, no smile, and no greeting for the boys. His voice is gruff and cold, like the three friends are criminals on the street.

As good of a cover story as Owen has thought of, Avery is beyond nervous right now. He's moved past the nervous stage and is in full blown panic. His voice is trapped in his throat because anger is not a look he sees on his father often, and Avery hates that it is currently directed at him.

Landon clears his throat. Both his father and Avery's look to him to speak up.

"It's kind of Owen's fault, but also, not really." He now stares at Owen wide eyed.

"Yeah, I mean, I just realized that the fireworks were coming. I asked Avery if he was ready to help Thor and Hulk through them because last year, they were a complete mess. He had no idea what I was talking about, of course, and I knew Officer Brown had those anxiety vests for them. Now, here we are," Owen says, offering an awe-shucks kind of smile.

"That explains intent, but not how you actually got into the house," says Avery's dad. The expression on his face has yet to change, arms are crossed over his chest, and Avery worries he is not buying any of this. Chief Fowler glues his eyes on Avery, who is now too afraid to speak.

"Well, we were already on this side of the island when I realized that I forgot the key that she had given us," says Landon. "Remember that, Dad?" He looks to his own father, his eyes wide with expectant hope.

Thankfully, Lt. Weatherby nods his head. "Yes, Brown gave us a key in case of emergencies. It's still on the hook in our kitchen."

"Yeah, so we just looked around hoping there was a spare key," says Owen, picking up his story telling from before, sounding as if this was all just totally natural, not a care in the world.

Chief Fowler still isn't lowering his guard. He hasn't moved, hasn't even let his eyes move from Avery. It's as if he can see the paranoia dripping from Avery's pores. Maybe he can.

"And you just, what?" asks Chief Fowler. "Scurried around in potted plants until you found a key? Picked the lock?"

Avery looks him straight in the eye. "She has the same gnome as Mom," Avery says, his voice strong and back straight. "I figured there was a key inside, and we thought that since technically Landon already had a key at home, it was kind of like permission. We didn't know that the house was going to look like this."

His dad's face softens, shoulders relax, and he nods his head.

"I have to call this in to the SBI. It was their crime scene, and I don't want it to seem like we are covering anything up. Before I place that call, I just need you guys to verify for me once again that you did not do this, and when I bring forensics in to check this out, they will not find your prints all over these frames and books and cushions or anything else that has been destroyed," Chief Fowler says.

They shake their heads no in response, much like young school children accepting a punishment.

"No, Dad, obviously we didn't tear apart her house. We didn't think it was still a crime scene. There was no sign or tape or anything. Why would we do this and then call you?" Avery protests.

The two police officers have still barely entered the house. Avery knows they want to preserve the crime scene as best as possible. Chief Fowler steps forward now and puts a hand on Avery's shoulder to settle him. His face is pained, but so is Avery's. Why does his dad seem to assume the worst about them?

"I'm sorry, Avery," Chief Fowler says gently. "I don't mean to seem like I am treating you like criminals. I know you have the best intentions, but something is obviously going on around here. This is our reputation on the line." He gestures between himself and Lt. Weatherby. "I just needed to be absolutely certain before I brought in another agency. I don't want any surprises. But I trust you."

He smiles slightly when he says that, and Avery's face lights up. Inside, though, he feels like a monster, because even though they did not wreck Officer Brown's house, he is lying to his dad. He doesn't deserve this trust, but it feels really good to have it.

"Weatherby, will you get forensics here?" asks the chief. "I am going to call my contact at the SBI. He will want to know that someone broke into the house of a deceased officer that allegedly harmed herself."

***

A group of men in polo shirts and khakis approach the house, bags and briefcases in hand.

"I am trying to imagine your dad dressed like that, Avery, and I can't for the life of me. It would be hilarious," Owen whispers.

"Yeah, well he prefers to be in the action, not cleaning up after it," Avery says, smiling. It doesn't bother him one bit that his dad isn't a polo shirt kind of guy.

The forensics crew doesn't seem to appreciate their whispering and laughter; two shoot a stony look in Owen's direction, the others huff at the fact that they have to walk around children to get into their crime scene.

One actually mutters, "Why are there children at my crime scene? They have no business being here."

Owen levels his eyes at the man, his cheeks red with anger. "Umm, that was our crime scene first. You people wouldn't even know there was a problem if it hadn't been for us. Maybe check yourself."

Avery is stunned. If he spoke that way to one of his dad's work associates, he wouldn't see the light of day again for a very long time. Maybe ever. But he also gets the frustration of always being discredited because of your age.

"Yeah, from what I understand, that is because you also made it a crime scene," retorts the man, referring to the fact that the boys were, on some technical level, trespassing.

"Whatever, we used a key," said Owen, not backing down a bit.

The forensics team go inside, loudly slamming the door behind them, a then stay out kind of move.

Landon chuckles softly. "Dude, you know he's gonna tell your dad."

"Let him," says Owen. "We didn't do anything wrong, even Avery's dad said so. Technically, we had permission, or at least you did. So those guys don't get to make us feel bad about, what? The fact that they have to do their jobs?"

Owen is on fire. Avery considers the differences between his two friends: Owen, the loud, athletic one never afraid to say what he feels or take a risk and Landon, the quiet, analytical one, the problem solver. What a pair they make. Avery's glad to know that whatever happens with soccer tomorrow, he still has them.

From their place on the porch, Avery observes his dad pacing in the backyard, covering his eyes out of frustration more than once with one hand while the other holds his phone. He wonders who is on the other end of the phone. Chief Fowler had said that they should be moving along, but Avery's not quite ready to abandon all that they had found.

"What do we do now?" Owen asks. "We can't just sit here. Those guys aren't going to share with us what they find. Ugh, what they find! Will they find it? Was all of this for nothing too? Why do we keep coming to dead ends!"

The license plate information from the music store's surveillance video, now the pictures of the plane. It is disappointing to not have been able to follow through on that, to not know for sure that they did something right to help Officer Brown.

Though, Avery isn't as upset as Owen because he knows his dad.

"You know, we're not going to get any kind of recognition, but we totally helped," says Avery. "Think about it, thanks to us, Andrew sent that video footage to my dad so that he would have it too. And I know my dad; he will find those pictures. If they are still there, I know he will."

"How can you know for sure?" Owen asks. "You had us move the desk to cover up the marks on the floor."

"Yeah, which might be the reason they are still there. But who do you think I learned that line of thinking from?"

Owen opens his mouth as if to argue back again, but then he closes it again. He stays quiet and just nods his head.

Out of nowhere, Landon pops up on his feet. His eyes are on the yard, no, beyond the yard. "Hey, Mrs. Fitzgerald! How are you?"

Avery looks over to where Landon's attention is and sees an older woman who is small in frame but wears a huge smile. Her white hair is piled high on her head and held in place with the help of a straw visor. She is dressed in loose fitting black shorts that come down to her knees and a pink button up short sleeved shirt, a strand of pearls around her neck. It seems odd that she would be dressed this way to dig in her garden, but she is. She stops what she is doing to walk over to the edge of her yard, and the boys get up to meet her where the yards meet.

"Why hello, Landon, Owen, and you, you must be Avery Fowler, dear, how are you? I'm Mrs. Fitzgerald," she says, outstretching her hand to shake his.

"We're doing alright, Mrs. Fitzgerald, but something very strange happened. It seems someone has broken in," explains Landon. And this is how news travels so fast in small towns, Avery learns.

Mrs. Fitzgerald covers her mouth for a moment, obviously surprised by his news. "Someone broke in? When? What could they possibly want from the poor woman?"

"We're not sure, ma'am," Avery says gently.

She nods, of course, because how could these children know, Avery assumes she is thinking, though she seems nice enough. "Why don't you boys come in for a little lemonade. You can tell me what you know, and we can try to figure this out."

She leads the way into her home, a small but immaculate beach cottage. Her kitchen is filled with color, the cabinets a shade of navy blue and the walls a pale aqua, the cushions on the kitchen chairs shades of blue. She has bouquets of flowers on the table and the counter, explosions of bright pinks and purples. It's a happy place, made even happier by all the pictures she has on the refrigerator of what must be grandchildren.

Mrs. Fitzgerald tells the boys to sit around the table, refusing their help while she pulls glasses down from the cabinet, takes a pitcher of lemonade from the fridge, places those items as well as a stack of plates on a tray to carry over to the table. She goes back over to the counter to acquire a stack of napkins and a cookie jar shaped like a Scottie dog.

"I made these chocolate chip cookies last night. They should still be fresh and tasty. You boys help yourself while I make a quick phone call."

They pour out lemonade and pass out cookies, even making Mrs. Fitzgerald a serving. Her phone calls all sounded the same: hey so and so, get over here. There's news about Officer Brown. Finally, she opens her back door and shouts Steve. Landon leans over to inform Avery that Steve is her husband.

Mrs. Fitzgerald sits at the table with the boys, taking a sip of her drink and thanking them for pouring it for her. A man with white hair comes in, a smile on his face despite the surprise guests at his kitchen table.

"Did my wife here recruit you boys to help us with some yard work?" he asks, stopping to rest a hand, still gloved from working outside, on the back of her chair. Avery wonders how this man isn't passing out from heat stroke in long sleeves, pants, and gloves.

"Why would I put them to work when I have you, dear? No, these boys told me that there was a break-in next door. I think we should figure out what is going on considering how close that is to our house. If we should be concerned," she explains.

There's a knock at the door, but neither adult goes to move, nor did they have to. The front door opens, Avery can hear it even though he can't see by whom. Voices float down the hallway from various women, all shouting hello and beginning with their questions immediately.

Three women come in, all older with graying hair to various degrees, in similar sundresses and large hats. Avery pieces together that they all live here, in the closest houses to Officer Brown.

Mrs. Fitzgerald introduces all the women to Avery, while Owen and Landon say their hellos and explain that their families are doing well; they even offer their seats to the women, though they are denied.

"Landon, your poor dad, having to find his partner like that. I should have sent something over to the house. I'm sure he is all shaken up," says a woman named Brenda, far taller than the other ladies.

Landon thanks her for the thought, but before he could say anything else, Mrs. Fitzgerald takes the conversation back. "Boys, let's start from the beginning. Let's help each other here. What were you doing in her house?"

With that, she nibbles a bite of a cookie and levels her eyes right on Avery. He shifts in his chair uncomfortably, the weight of all these older people's eyes making him nervous, and he hopes that Landon or Owen will speak up. But he looks at each of them, and they seem content to let him take the lead.

Avery takes a sip of his lemonade, then begins his story. "We are here for the dogs, actually. Owen remembered that they get anxiety during fireworks, and with the Fourth only a few days away, we thought we better get their anxiety vests. We didn't see any police tape, and Landon had a key, so we went in."

One of the women makes a noise in her throat, it sounded out of irritation. Steve adds one of his own, as if to agree with her. Avery couldn't keep the confusion off his face.

"There was never any police tape. The investigators moved in and out of there pretty quickly," Mrs. Fitzgerald adds.

"Really?" Avery is shocked. He knows from his father's stories how long searching a house can take, how thorough police officers should be.

"Honey, they didn't even talk to a single one of us, despite the fact that we were Diana's neighbors and knew allllllllll of her comings and goings. They didn't seem to think our input was needed, other than my Joe, and that was really just to find out about the state of the house when he went in and took the dogs. How are they doing, by the way?" said a woman whose name Avery thinks is Cheryl. He's only trying to focus on what is important, and names don't fit that today. He's trying to think how he can sneak a few questions in, what would be helpful, what would they actually tell a group of kids.

However, he didn't need to ask a single thing. That's how town gossips work, apparently.

Avery listens as he hears about how her family had not visited for a while, and that made the neighbors worry. How it was sometimes hard to keep up with her schedule because she worked so much, she seemed obsessed with work. One woman discloses how a man used to be over there all the time, and then, abruptly, that ended. None of them ever heard any arguing, and while they have seen the two of them together since, it has never been at the house as they were doing the "just friends thing". The boys nod like they understand what that means, but Avery's knowledge of relationships is nonexistent, and he has no idea what she's talking about.

When the women say all there is for them to say, Mr. Fitzgerald clears his throat and begins, "My addition isn't as much fun as what the ladies had to offer. I would see Officer Brown out in her backyard at night, after dark, often. She would have the dogs out there with her, yes, but she wouldn't be paying attention to them. Her eyes were up, her whole attention was up, as though she were looking for something. And, well, this is just speculation, but there is a big section of time when she seemed very unhappy. Her smile wasn't as big or as bright, and she left her house less. However, that stopped a few weeks before she passed away. Those weeks she was back to her vibrant self."

She seemed sad, and according to her journals, she had been, Avery thinks. Work was hard, she had no support, and she felt as though something illegal was happening and no one would help her uncover it, not because it was too dangerous, but because whatever was happening, money was more important.

A quiet falls over the group. The cookies are gone, lemonade at its last.

Mrs. Fitzgerald looks at the boys, keeping her eyes on the face of each boy for a moment. "Alright fellas, we shared ours. Now you tell us, do we have anything to be worried about?"

She has no idea what a difficult question she is asking. Avery would like to answer it for this sweet woman. If Officer Brown was right, and this whole large illegal operation is happening in their town, who knows what that could mean for the locals. But the boys don't know for sure if she is right, and to get this group riled up over what could be nothing seems dangerous, not to mention how angry his dad would be.

"We have no idea who did this or what they were looking for," Avery says.

"Ohhhh!" says Brenda, clapping her hands like a lightning bolt struck her brain. "You know what I heard! That boy, what's his name. The one's who's always been trouble with a capital T."

"The Callaway boy?" asks Mrs. Fitzgerald.

"Yes! That's the one. Apparently, he got himself arrested for breaking into the police department and stealing evidence. Rumor has it he was paid to do it."

"Paid by whom?" Mr. Fitzgerald asks.

Avery wonders how often he gets caught listening to these women go back and forth with their stories, like a crazed tennis match that has more than two competitors.

Brenda turns her head to Mr. Fitzgerald and answers, "Well, that I don't know. Yet."

While the other women began chatting again, Mrs. Fitzgerald tells the boys she would see them out. She opens the front door for them, but then follows them out onto the porch, closing the door behind them. A smile still sits on her face, but it is much smaller, tighter now. Sadness swims in her eyes, a single tear flows down her cheek.

"Thank you, boys, for sharing that information with us and for taking care of Thor and Hulk," she says. "I loved Officer Brown; she was always the first one to come to my aide. I will make sure we keep an eye on the house. If we see anything, we will call one of your fathers. Please let me know if we can help with whatever you are up to."

They smile bashfully and thank her. Landon tells her to be sure to come and see them at the soccer games, and she promises she will. Then the boys make their way down the walk and start back towards the other side of the island.

"See, Owen. We are doing something right," says Avery. "That kid was arrested."

He can't help but smile and looks to see that his friends wear the exact same one.

"Yeah," Landon says. "We did make that happen, didn't we?"

Chapter 19

Sadly, dinner feels like normal. Avery keeps his mom company in the kitchen. They opened the doors and windows so that the sound of the ocean is audible over the 90s soundtrack Mrs. Fowler has playing. The sun is still up in the sky, the beach littered with families trying to enjoy the last few minutes of each day before they have to travel home, the squeals of the children floating up to their back porch and into their kitchen.

While she cooks, Avery tells his mother everything that has happened, finding it hard to believe that it all occurred in a single day. He even tells her about the little old ladies with their endless skills of observation. His mom laughed at that, reminding him that in small towns people pay attention to one another, and it isn't necessarily a bad thing. He told her what Mr. Fitzgerald said about Officer Brown being sad up until a few weeks before her death.

She stops stirring her vegetable medley and turns down the heat at that moment to give Avery her full attention. "Do you think that coincides with when we arrived, specifically when it is clear your father, former VICE agent, was going to be taking over the department? Is that what you think Mr. Bowen was hinting at?"

Avery doesn't answer the question because a new question pops into his mind. "Do you think that's why Dad brought us here? Did he know that all of this is going on in this town? Was it not really about us being a family, but more about him getting this huge bust?"

He doesn't mean to sound so angry, but this conclusion, this accusation really, has made its way to the front of his mind, and he feels like he can't ignore it. It seems so obvious; his father is way too young to want to kick back in this tired beach town. He has too much drive, too much passion for what he does to be happy here. From the military, to the streets, to this cushy desk job; it is a natural progression, but way too fast.

His dad said this decision is about family time, about being home for dinners and soccer games and family vacations. It's too much of a coincidence that he didn't know this was going on.

Avery can feel the emotions rushing to his face, the redness filling his cheeks. He is angry, and what is worse, is that yet again his father isn't here for him to talk to. So much for family dinners.

His mother walks over to Avery's side of the counter and takes his face into her hands gently. She holds his head up, forcing him to make eye contact. "I want you to hear these words, kid. I see you are upset. I understand it, but you need to talk to your father before you let these emotions consume you. Your father is a good man, but you already know that. If he said that we came down here to pursue a quieter life, we came down here to have a quieter life. Have faith in your father, Avery."

Each word is soft, meant to soothe and calm. Avery nods, which is difficult to do while his mother still has possession of his face. The redness leaves his cheeks, and the realization comes that he has jumped to a lot of conclusions. His mom kisses the top of his head before turning to go back to the stove.

"Maybe we take a break from police talk tonight. I know, it's deeply ingratiated in our lives, but let's talk about anything else in the world. Let's just be happy," she suggests.

Dinner smells good, and it is a beautiful evening, so Avery agrees. They talk about design ideas for his bedroom, the kind of furniture he would like, paint options.

"Mom, what is it that you do all day long? I mean, you move to this new place with no friends, and yet you still seem..."

"Mysterious? Elusive?" she laughs. "I stay busy, bear, because I like to be busy. I am a real person. I love being your mom, but you're growing up. You need me less. And I've made friends, starting with Landon and Owen's moms, but also some of the other teachers from your school that I will be working with. I've also been meeting with a publisher."

"A publisher for what?" he asks. His head feels like it could explode. Who is this woman before him? He actually feels pretty badly that he always thinks about all of the cool things his dad does, and he forgets that his mom is this pretty amazing human.

His mom brightens at the question, her eyes shining as she explains that she's finished a book of poetry and illustrations, and there is some interest in it.

"Mom, that's awesome. I'm proud of you," he says.

"Thank you, bear," she says, her eyes looking a little wet. "I'm proud of you, too. No matter what happens tomorrow, I will always be your biggest fan."

She reaches over and squeezes his hand, and Avery feels relaxed and content for the first time in a few days, but he still wishes his father were home.

***

His dad came home sometime during the night, as evidenced by the clean dinner plate washed and left on the drying rack. His father can never just leave a dish to be done later. It's a thing Avery knows about his dad, just like he knows his mother is right about needing to trust in his father. But he isn't ready to just let it go. It seems all a little too convenient.

Talking to the chief would have been helpful, but he came home late and left early, the plate the only indication that Avery could see. He stares at it while chewing the eggs his mother made him, her voice is hanging in the room, but his thoughts dominate his brain, no room for any other interruptions.

"Okay, good talk," says his mom, clearly irritated.

Avery shovels another bite of eggs into his mouth and shrugs his shoulders.

"Yeah, that's what I am talking about. Hey, get your head in the game. You're going to be great today! Do you want me to go with you to the tryouts?"

Avery stops chewing and stares at her, eyes wide, mouth straight, total disbelief radiating from him.

"I love you, but no, I don't need my mommy to take me to soccer."

She comes over to him and grabs his face, laying big kisses all over his head and face, making exaggerated sounds with each one.

"Mom! Stop! You're loving me to death!" he says through his laughter.

She lets him go, and they laugh together for a few moments.

"You'll be great today. I can feel it," she whispers before kissing his head and turning her attention to the dishes.

***

Music pumping through his headphones, Avery does his best to clear his head before meeting with Coach Gilmore. No room for worrying about his dad's job or his intentions or what happened to Officer Brown. The only thing he can afford to worry about in this moment is making his way on the school's soccer team.

He leaves his bike just where he had yesterday and walks onto the field. Coach isn't here yet, so Avery takes a few moments to stretch his legs, pulling on his quad muscles and letting his calf muscles warm up. All he can hear are his deep breaths, the breeze, and the birds. It's peaceful and soothing, the sun not yet to its peak position in the sky.

"Hey, Avery," says Coach Gilmore.

Avery tumbles from his quad stretch; his face goes white, eyes wide in shock, hands now on his heart.

"Oh, man, I am so sorry. I didn't mean to startle you," Coach Gilmore says. "You must have been zoned out to have not heard the truck or anything."

"Yeah, I was. Or at least I was trying to be," says Avery. "I wanted to show you that I deserve a place on the team. I really appreciate you offering me this second attempt."

"It's not a problem. I imagine you have a lot on your mind, what with moving to a whole new town, then there being a murder in that new town. It must be scary, especially considering how close your dad is to it all," says the coach. "And speaking of your dad, he sent me an email last night, and it included some video from some of your games from your last school. He said that when you want it, you go for it. So the question is, Avery, do you want this? Are you ready to go all in?"

Avery's cheeks are red, unsure of how to feel about what his dad did for him. Part of him thinks it's awesome that his dad was willing to speak up for him, and the other part of him is a little embarrassed. But he can't think of all the complicated thoughts and emotions he feels about his dad right now. He's got to prove himself because two months ago, no, he wasn't ready to go all in on anything other than his video games and tacos. Now, though, he realized how quickly life changes and how quickly you can lose things and people. He wants to be someone who cares like Officer Brown did, who stays busy and passionate like his mom, who believes in hard work and dedication like his dad.

"Yes, sir. I am all in."

Coach explains that they will run the drill from yesterday again, putting Avery in the position of offense. Avery dribbled the ball down the field, nimble, small kicks, his eyes moving quickly between the coach and the ball. A quick scissor and move to his left and somehow, he was around Coach. Now he sprints, tapping the ball ahead of him, moving into position to score. He pounds the ball with the center of his foot and sends it soaring into the goal, the swish of the net audible.

"Beautiful!" yells the coach. "Do it again!"

***

The water in Landon's pool is like bath water: warm and comforting. The crystal blue water laps up on Avery as he relaxes on the huge float shaped like a hot pink flamingo, his head reclined back against its neck. The sun reflects off the water, and it's so hot you can see the heat radiating above the deck surrounding the pool. But Avery has his sunglasses on, a smoothie in his hand, some top 40 hits playing, and his friends around him. It's perfect.

"Cannon ball!" yells Owen just before his body pounds the water, sending droplets flying and waves that cause Landon and Avery's floats to bob like buoys in the ocean. Owen's head comes back to the surface, and he smiles at the aftermath.

"I don't understand why we are sitting here talking about this investigation or whatever instead of planning how to celebrate.

Bro! You made it on the team! Let's do something!" Owen says.

"Owen, we have plenty of time to do that," Landon answers, his voice sounding an awful lot like a teacher who has dealt with kindergarteners all day. "This investigation, though, has an expiration date. Get your head in the game."

"Man, my head is in the game! Watch yourself," Owen says. "But what can we really do right now? I mean, according to Miss Brenda, our boy got arrested thanks to our smart thinking. We can't do a thing about the license plate situation or about the plane unless you're ready just to walk up to Mr. Ramsey and ask him if he's flying his plane around like a wackadoodle and maybe killing people off. And I'm sure he'll just tell us all about it."

"Well with that attitude, obviously he will," says Avery, rolling his eyes. "You're not wrong about the car and the plane. I think it's super suspect that Mr. Ramsey is the one who owns the plane, and now he's the one whose store gets broken into."

"Or maybe you just want to see a connection where there actually isn't one," says Landon before taking a huge gulp of his smoothie. Avery shoots him a look, so he holds his hands up and says "Hey, it's possible that it's completely random."

"Yeah, yeah, but it's also possible that it isn't," Avery says. "And if it isn't, it means he's involved in some sort of drug scandal, according to Mr. Bowen and Officer Brown."

"Okay, I want more information on that because it's just bananas to me that we wouldn't know about it," Owen demands. "Landon, where's your phone or tablet or whatever gadget you got? Let's look it up, see if there's any kind of information about Summerset Island and drugs."

Avery thinks about the conversation he had with his mom last night. Officer Brown thought that narcotics had a large presence in this area. How could Avery's father not have been aware of that?

Landon rolls off of his float and paddles to the side of the pool, reaching for his phone. Avery anchors himself beside Landon, who types in a generic search for southeast NC and narcotics. Avery sees Landon's eyes go wide at the results.

The screen is full of titles like After a Four Month Investigation, Twenty-Two Are Arrested in Craven County for Drug Distribution, Vacant Farmland Found to Be the Home of Drug Manufacturing, Wilmington Man Federally Charged in Drug Ring, and Separate Investigations Lead to the Arrest of a Trio on Trafficking Charges. Avery looks at the dates; these news headlines only went back for three months, and there were countless more to follow.

Landon clicks on a few of the articles, summarizing each one for Owen and Avery so that they didn't have to try to share a small screen. In each account, thousands upon thousands of dollars of narcotics were seized, the arrested participants receiving charges like trafficking, intent to traffic, maintaining a dwelling for a controlled substance, and of course, many also dealt with possession of illegal firearms.

"This might be a stupid question, but what is trafficking? How is that different from just selling drugs?" Owen asks. Avery forgets that his family conversations are probably very different from those of other people.

"It's basically like moving the product from one place to another. But traffickers will bring it to those who plan to sell it, I think," says Avery. "So it's like they work together, but the charges are different due to state lines and the amount of drugs."

"Then Officer Brown wasn't worried about people just selling, was she?" Owen asks, connecting a lot of dots thanks to the information on the screen in front of him.

"I think if she was out at the lighthouse in the middle of the night, watching people in planes with huge bags of money or drugs, no," says Landon very quietly. "She was looking for the bigger fish."

The boys sit in silence for a minute. Avery considers what this means for his dad, his safety, and his reasons for coming here.

"Hey, this is totally random, but what are the odds your parents have a paper map of the area?" Avery asks Landon.

"Uhh, pretty good, actually," Landon says. "My dad hates using his phone to navigate anything. He says only the weak do that. Let me grab one from the garage." He pushes his hands against the deck and hoists himself out of the water, walking in the direction of the garage.

"Grab a pen, too," Avery shouts after him.

Landon returns with both requested items. The boys sit around a table, towels wrapped around their waists. Avery smooths the map out on the table and takes the pen in his hand.

"Okay, read to me the town names," says Avery. "Give me repeats, too, and I can tally them."

Landon starts calling out town names: Wilmington, Ash, Porter's Neck, New Bern, Fayetteville, Leland, the list went on and on. Avery had him widen the search, asking him to go back a few years, even decades. Landon broadened the search for the type of crime. Some offences were minor, and some were huge, but by the time Landon makes it to the end of the last list, Avery's point is clear.

Owen and Landon stand on either side of Avery, the map laid out in front of them. There isn't a single town or city that escapes without some mention of drugs, even the simplest infraction. There isn't a single one, of course, except Summerset Island.

"So we are supposed to believe that there is a bubble around the island that keeps bad things and bad people out?" Owen asks.

"No, I think the bad people are very obviously here," Avery says under his breath.

"Worse. I think the bad people are very obviously in charge," says Landon, his tone never more worried. "Here's one more that I didn't mention; it's not about a drug bust, it's about an election. Five years ago, there was a newly elected district attorney. He ran his whole campaign talking about how he was going to clear out the drugs in the entire county and get rid of the corruption. A few months into his time as DA, he was killed in a car accident. They say that his steering was tampered with."

Landon's tan face looks pale despite his hours in the sun, and even sarcastic Owen has nothing to say to this. It's hard not to be worried by this information. But what can they do with it?

Chapter 20

"Well super! Here's more information that's really disturbing, yet we can do nothing with or about it," says Owen. He collapses back into his seat and squints up into the sky.

"Alright, so, we think Mr. Ramsey has something to do with this drug problem, right? And that his store being broken into seems suspicious?" asks Landon.

Avery turns his head to look at Landon with a deadpan expression, and with a flat tone says, "Oh, now you want to believe that there is a connection."

"Whatever, shut up," says Landon. "We don't have many break-ins, but now the police station and Mr. Ramsey's store have been broken into. Is it possible it's by the same person? Or, more accurately, the same group of people. I find it hard to believe that Brendan Callaway worked completely alone. I mean, if one of us were going to commit a crime, wouldn't we tell each other?"

"I mean, yeah, probably, but his friends aren't just going to talk to us," Avery says.

"Duh. But they aren't the sharpest tools in the shed, so maybe they will be running their mouths about whatever happened, especially if only Brendan gets arrested for it," says Landon.

"Would they do that if they saw you guys hanging around?"

Avery asks.

"Oh, they have no idea who we are. We're just middle school losers or whatever," says Landon.

"Orrrr we could save a whole lot of time, and Avery could go bat his eyelashes at Marissa again," says Owen, laughing and wiggling his eyebrows.

"Dude, no," says Avery, wishing he had something to throw at Owen. "I don't want to do that. She seems nice."

"Alright, well what other card do we have?" Landon asks. His voice sounded exasperated, and Avery understands why. They have been trying so hard, but things keep slipping through their reach.

"Who's the doctor again? You know, the one that said that it seemed like a good possibility Officer Brown did this to herself?" asks Avery.

Owen stretches his arms into the air, the excitement finding its way back into his eyes. "Ahhh, I forgot about that information. His name came up twice at the police station, right? And the SBI really seemed to listen to him. Amando is his name. What about him? He definitely won't talk to us," says Owen.

"Well, no, but maybe we only need him to talk to one of us, while the rest of us try to figure out what he had to gain by lying about Officer Brown," Avery says. "This is a terrible idea, so if you say no, I get it, but it's the only idea I've got."

"Out with it then," says Owen, a gleam in his eye.

***

"So, you think it could work? Spying on Dr. Amando and seeing if he leads us to Mr. Ramsey?" asks Avery.

They are riding their bikes in the center of the road, as usual. Landon's mom was bustling about in the kitchen, grumbling about dinner time, and Avery and Owen felt it was time to hit the road.

The summer sun is still high in the sky despite the hour, and Avery tries to focus on the warmth of his skin and not how nervous he is about his plan, which is the most reckless thing they have done yet, especially considering how loud Owen usually is.

"I'm down. I don't see what other choice we have right now. Not if you want to leave Marissa out of it," says Owen.

"Dude, leave her out of it!" Avery says, but he can hear Owen humming something about sitting in a tree, k-i-s-s-i-n-g. "You're so lame!"

His stomach is starting to hurt he's laughing so hard. He has to stop pedaling to make sure he doesn't fall over. They have made it to the business section of the island, and Avery looks up to see exactly where they are. The building is a pale blue with white shutters, meant to look like a house though it is not one. The sign in front advertises the real estate business.

All of a sudden, the door swings open aggressively, and a man storms out quickly despite the fact that his arms are filled with boxes. He makes it to the SUV sitting out front with his tower of boxes, but as he tries to open the back hatch, the top box leans precariously to the side, finally toppling over completely.

In frustration, the man yells out, and Owen turns to see what the commotion is.

"Oh, that's Mr. Fountain. He recently left the island, though he used to be one of the big dogs around here," whispers Owen. "Maybe we should go help him."

Avery agrees, and they push their bikes over to him, Owen calling out a hello. Mr. Fountain looks up with a sharp jerk of his head, his eyes expectant and wide. He must not have realized people were around.

"Hey, Mr. Fountain. Need some help?" Owen asks.

Sheepishly, the man says yes, looking at his possessions on the ground. When he looks up again, it's directly at Avery. His brown hair is mostly gray, but he wears a well-fitting navy suit that is currently pretty rumpled.

"I apologize. I don't think I know you," says Mr. Fountain. He sticks his hand out in greeting; "Rick Fountain," he says in a deep voice.

Avery reaches his hand out first to shake the man's, stating his full name just as Mr. Fountain had.

"Avery Fowler; yes, I can see that. I don't know if you are aware of this, son, but I am the reason your father is here."

Avery looks at this man with intense interest. "What does that mean, exactly?"

"I reached out to him. I have family that lives in Ocean City, New Jersey, and your dad's name was constantly in the news there. No pictures, of course, but enough for me to be able to send him an email and invite him down here," Mr. Fountain explains while the three of them squat around his boxes, picking up his items and replacing them in their box. "Officer Brown, she had asked me for help. She came to me, so upset about planes and these theories. She said the department needed leadership."

"So you told my dad about the job?" Avery asks, thinking back to Mr. Bowen's story and his own suspicion that maybe his dad didn't come here just to relax. "Did he know why you brought him here?"

Mr. Fountain shakes his head. Then he glances up, looking all around. He seems cautious, even a little frightened. He stands and grabs his boxes roughly, shoving them into the back of his SUV. "I'm sorry, I've said too much. Please tell your father I'm sorry. I'm so sorry that I failed her. I've got to get off this island. Be careful boys."

He rushes around to the driver's side door.

"Hey, be careful of what?" Owen shouts after him.

But it's too late. Mr. Fountain starts the car and drives off, squealing his tires as he goes.

"Is it just me, or was that really weird?" asks Owen.

"He was afraid of something, right? Did you see that?" Avery asks.

"Yeah, but what is there to be afraid of?" asks Owen.

Avery looks around them. The ocean is just off in the distance, its smell comforting. This island is so picture perfect, but why does he keep finding the ugliest sides of it?

Chapter 21

The driveway is empty, which catches Avery by surprise because it is dinner time, and by the looks of it, there is no one home to feed him. The lights in the front of the house shine out the window, though, so someone has been home recently.

He pushes his bike up the driveway and leans it against the garage for now. He walks up the steps to the porch, looking in the windows as he goes, digging in his backpack for his keys which seem to be lost somewhere in the bottom of it. He checks the handle to see if it's open, so he can stop this manic search. Thankfully, the handle pushes all the way down, and he makes his way inside.

The house is quiet. A few weeks ago, that would not be a surprise, but now it is. The sound of two bounding dogs should be filling Avery's ears, but it isn't. The dogs are nowhere to be seen. He knows his dad would not have taken them to the police station, and if his dad isn't home, then that must be where he is. And his mom would not put those two big dogs in her Jeep, not unless there's an emergency and she needed to squeeze them in.

Avery crosses the house to the kitchen, the lights on in there as well. He sees a note from his mother, telling him that she ran out for one more thing for his room, but that when she returns, she will have dinner with her, not to worry. Avery turns back to survey the house, but everything looks normal. He tells himself too much has been happening lately, he's letting things get to his head, but he knows he would feel better if the dogs were around, so he shouts for them.

A huge bang causes Avery to duck and swing around simultaneously. It's nothing but those two knuckleheaded dogs, though, their paws crashing against the door as they stand on their hind legs and try to get in. Avery walks over and opens the door for them.

"How did you two get out there, huh?" he asks, bending and petting their heads while they lick his face in hello. Avery feels a lot better now, but he closes and secures the door behind him. No need for more surprises tonight.

He turns to walk to his room, fighting to maneuver against the dogs who are jumping and all riled up. "I know, guys, I know. You shouldn't have been left outside, but you have to let me walk." He tries to take a few more steps, but the dogs are still hindering his path. "Seriously! Cool it, boys. At ease!"

He makes it to his room, the dogs still trailing at his feet but at least they allow him to walk. His door is closed, which is odd because he normally leaves it open, but what about tonight hasn't been odd? He opens the door and can see a pile of stuff in the center of his room, bags and boxes, things that his mom went out and acquired today in order to update Avery's space. He turns on the light to get a better look at the loot that his mom has delivered.

But he can barely keep a bag open; the dogs keep shoving their heads in his way, manically trying to get his attention.

"Look guys, I know it's weird that Mom left you outside, but what are you getting so pushy with me for?" asks Avery. They don't stop though.

Avery starts to get a sinking feeling in his stomach, that something isn't exactly as it should be. He wishes he had a cell phone, or at least a phone in his room. He reaches for the Magic 8-Ball in its home beside his bed, shakes it and asks, "Am I just being silly, or is there something wrong?"

Yes.

Avery's heart pounds inside his chest, the sound of it vibrating in his ears. The dogs are circling his legs, and while moments ago they brought him comfort, now all he can feel is panic. His breathing quickens while he tries to think of what to do. He looks back at the ball in his hand.

"Is someone else here now?" he says, barely above a whisper.

He turns the ball back over, the window showing the message, You may rely on it.

Avery turns to walk back out of his room, back out the front door, but again the dogs are blocking him. He can barely walk. He's barely taken a handful of steps when he sees something else in his way: the figure of a man, a man who is without question not his father.

Avery's eyes go wide, his breath caught in his chest. Panic rolls over him in waves, and he feels like he is glued to where he stands. Somehow, he finds his voice.

"Someone help, help me please!" he screams at the top of his lungs, hoping that the neighbors can hear him, hoping that the waves are not too wild tonight, so loud that they will swallow his cries whole before they can reach the ears of anyone who might be close enough to save him. Avery keeps shouting, the hooded figure coming towards him, though Avery cannot hear the sounds of his shoes on the ground, cannot hear if the man is saying anything. He can hear nothing over the sound of his heart, not even his own voice pleading for help. Because while he sees the man, sees the hood, more importantly, he sees the gleaming object the man holds in his hand: a knife, long and sharp, a knife intended to do Avery harm.

Avery looks around his room to see if there is anything he can use to defend himself. He sees nothing, though, no baseball bat, no BB gun, and thanks to his mom's work, there's not even a chair to use against this stranger with ill intent. Avery rushes to his window, hoping he can get it open in time, somehow get out of it before this man can do whatever he is going to do. He opens the locks and is pushing with all his strength against the glass, trying to move it up, still shouting, still pushing. And then he hears it, someone else's scream. Avery turns from the window to see that Thor has latched on to the man's arm, the one not holding the knife.

The man howls in pain, but Avery yells for Thor and Hulk, afraid of what might happen to them. They do not listen, though.

Thor holds strong, and Hulk stands in front of Avery barking with all the ferocity he has in him.

And now there is a new noise; the front door is open, and Avery can hear his mother calling for him. He yells to warn her not to come in here, that there's a knife, but his voice is muffled over the sound of Thor's squalls of pain. The blood stains his fur quickly, and he runs to Avery having let go of the arm.

A hood, a bandana, Avery can see no face, but he hears the man's voice clearly, "Tell your father we don't want him here."

The man runs from the bedroom, slamming into Mrs. Fowler as she tries to make her way to Avery, shoving her so hard she pounds into the wall behind her and is momentarily stunned. She runs after him, but he is gone, the back door wide open. The hooded man leaps the fence and takes off down the beach.

Mrs. Fowler gives up her chase, takes her cell phone out of her back pocket, and dials 911 while she walks to the bathroom linen closet for towels. The dispatcher picks up immediately: "911, what is your emergency?"

Mrs. Fowler is back in Avery's room, side stepping droplets of blood and ensuring the preservation of evidence, taking one towel from the stack, dropping to her knees, and applying pressure to Thor's wound. She kisses the top of his head and says, "We are located on 562 Seashell Way and need immediate police and paramedic response. We have a stab victim, but we were unable to contain the intruder. He ran out the back door down the beach, to the south of the island. You need to alert people to lock their doors. And I need help, now please."

Her eyes run over Avery as she speaks. There are no visible cuts, no bruises, he does not seem to be bleeding, he is still standing, all of these things should be telling her that he is okay, he is okay, but he isn't okay. Someone tried to attack him.

The dispatcher tells her to stay calm because help is on the way, but Mrs. Fowler is as calm as a mother could be given what she walked into. She grabs another towel to put on top of the first, and finally, now that the police have been called and she feels like she is doing all she can for Thor, she looks directly in Avery's eyes and asks if he is hurt.

He crouches down by her, offering Thor his hand, scratching his ears with one hand and keeping the other on Hulk, letting them both know they are good boys. "Yeah, Mom, I am fine."

"No, Avery, you are not fine," she says. "You were just attacked. Your dogs, dogs that we wouldn't have had if it weren't for a tragedy, just had to save your life. One of them is lying in a puddle of blood. I am not fine. You cannot be fine, and you don't need to pretend as though you are. Talk to me."

Avery sees the pain in Thor's eyes, he sees Hulk cowering, and he can't do anything to explain to them what happened, why this happened. He shakes his head, "I can't talk right now, Mom. I don't know the words right now." He can see from her pinched mouth and watery eyes that she is upset, so he apologizes.

Her brows furrow. "Avery, you have nothing to apologize for. I am just so... relieved that I made it here when I did. I would never forgive myself if something had happened to you."

Sirens interrupt her words, a lot of them. The cavalry's here. Over all of the noise, sirens, voices, Avery can hear his father.

"Dad, we're back here!" Avery responds, not willing to leave Thor. By now, his mom has put four towels on him. Into the doorway rushes Chief Fowler, pausing at the entryway to take note of what has happened, what the clues tell him. He carefully makes his way to Avery and wraps his arms around him. Then he brings his radio to his lips and tells the EMTs to come to the bedroom at the hallway's end.

A man and woman enter the hallway, light blue shirts contrasting with the all-black police uniforms, their hands filled with satchels of medical equipment, a gurney left at the end of the hallway. Chief Fowler tells them to be sure not to touch anything; he won't allow for another crime scene to be tampered with on his watch. The woman scans the scene, quickly realizing that Avery has not been severely injured, nor his mother. She is not amused. "We're not veterinarians," she says, gesturing to Thor who didn't even startle at their arrival.

Mrs. Fowler doesn't even turn to look at the woman. "Look, I know this isn't exactly following protocol, but you can treat animals. Nowhere in your handbook or whatever it is you have does it say that you cannot treat animals, especially when the animal was injured in the actual police emergency. He saved my son, and because he did so, he is injured. We are in the middle of nowhere. Summerset does not have a 24-hour animal hospital. It will take me time to get the vet here. I don't have time, but I do have you. So please, do what you can."

Maybe it is Mrs. Fowler's words, maybe it is the fact that the chief of police sits there with judgement written all over his face, but the two ask for the family to step aside so that they can get to work. They agree, and Mrs. Fowler takes Hulk into the back yard. His barking at the paramedics would only slow them down.

The room is a disaster, the boxes and bags his mom had piled neatly in his room trampled, blood on the floor, and far too many people. When his father signals him to follow, Avery happily does.

"Tell me exactly what happened, leaving absolutely nothing out," says his dad, pressing the record button on his phone. Avery does as he's told, detailing the empty driveway, the unlocked front door, his mom's note, the quietness because the dogs had been put outside, how they were blocking his way, but he thought they just wanted attention, not that they were trying to stop him.

He is speaking quickly, each sentence and detail running after each other. He's obviously still overcome with panic, despite the fact that the danger is gone. Or at least it is for now. Avery describes the man wearing a hood, how Avery didn't see the knife at first, how he had nothing to defend himself with, so he tried the window, and then all of a sudden Thor was protecting him and Hulk moved between Avery and the intruder, then Mrs. Fowler bursting in and trying to catch up to the guy.

"Your mother chased after him?" asks his dad. The look on his face is priceless.

"Yeah, but he got a jump on her because he shoved her into the wall. When she realized that she wasn't going to be able to do anything, she called you guys and started to work on Thor," Avery says.

"You guys know that I am the police officer in the family, right? Not the two of you? What is your mother thinking, going after some stranger that broke into the house?" He's shaking his head back and forth as though he can move the thoughts into places that make sense.

"I think she was thinking someone broke into her house, and she wasn't here for it," says Avery. "She didn't hesitate. And if it makes you feel better, the guy only shoved her to get past her; he never swung at her or anything like that."

"Yeah, yeah, I feel so much better now. What am I going to do with that woman?" A voice calls from another room, something about how she deserves a vacation. A laugh escapes Avery's lips; only his mother would be able to hear their conversation from that far away, the hearing power of both a mother and a teacher.

"There's one more thing, Dad," Avery says, the laughter completely gone from his voice. "The guy, he said they didn't want you here."

Avery watches his dad's face, but there is no response. He's in full-blown work mode now. He won't be revealing anything.

"Okay, bud. Thanks for telling me. Don't worry. We will catch this guy," says the chief.

Chief Fowler makes sure that everything is documented: a

description of the man, his black standard hoodie and bandana covering his face, slightly taller than Avery's mother; the blood on the ground, both Thor's and the intruder's; the indentions on the wall from where Mrs. Fowler hit her head and elbow so hard. The paramedics offered to take a look at her, too, that she may have a concussion, but she waved them off.

Summerset Island's one and only veterinarian is at the house, and with the help of the two paramedics, he stitches Thor up, warning that this is the easy part. The hard part will be making sure Thor takes it easy and doesn't pull any stitches. He is lucky. Avery is lucky.

With the blood sample safely sent off to be tested and the fingerprints taken from Avery's bedroom door and the back door, Lt. Weatherby arrives to force them all to pack a bag. With the help of the paramedics, they got Thor in the back of Chief Fowler's truck, Hulk standing guard over him. The Fowler family follows the lieutenant's truck to his home where a warm dinner is waiting, and crime tape doesn't exist.

Chapter 22

Landon's house is very different from Avery's. Mrs. Fowler likes things to feel bright and airy, while this house feels very... not. The living room is neat and masculine due to its wood paneling, lined with bookcases with well-loved novels and coffee table books laying down to fit the shelf. There are pictures of fishing trips and hiking expeditions and things that Avery is sure are not called knick knacks by their owners, but he doesn't know what else to call them. Two large armchairs have their backs to the kitchen, and they face a worn leather couch. The couch sits in front of an expansive window that lacks blinds. The sheer curtains make the room bright and welcoming in the daytime, but it's late, so the room is just dark in many ways.

The conversation should have been about sleeping arrangements. They should have been discussing whether the boys would be in the same homeroom. Instead, the conversation is about keeping the boys safe. Avery didn't see this coming. He's also not very happy about it. This never would have happened in New Jersey.

The dining room table is mostly empty aside from cast off coffee cups and empty ice cream bowls, as if ice cream could make people forget exactly what occurred tonight. Owen has joined them, though his father is still out on the beach patrolling, looking for a man whose arm should be bandaged from a dog bite.

"I think I can speak for all of the adults when I say you boys need to stick close to home," says Chief Fowler.

"But Dad, home isn't safe anymore either. We're not even allowed to be there," says Avery.

"What I think your dad means is that we need to know where you are," says Lt. Weatherby. "I know you guys tell us when you leave, but we also know you sometimes wander from one place to the next without thinking about checking in. Now, you need to think about checking in."

"Better than think about it, you better do it. Especially you, Landon. You have a phone, so no excuses," says Mrs. Weatherby.

Avery fidgets in his chair. He doesn't want to admit this in front of his friends, but he doesn't want to leave his parents' sight for the foreseeable future. If his mom hadn't come home, what would have happened? He doesn't want to think like that, but he can't not think like that.

"Avery, are you okay?" his mom asks him. She's sitting across the table from him, and Avery can see the fear reflected in her eyes.

"No, not really. And maybe it's time we wonder if coming here was a mistake," Avery says in a whisper. He doesn't want to hurt Owen and Landon's feelings, but let's not forget that he never wanted to move in the first place. Now, in the span of only a few weeks, he's had someone close to him die, his father is being pushed out of his job, and Avery's been attacked, his home intruded upon and violated. Yeah, maybe it's time to go.

"It's been a lot, Avery, I know. Being scared is only normal; in fact, I would be worried if you weren't scared," says his mom. "But running away never solves anything. We've decided that this is our home now. Besides, your father could never walk away with all these open investigations, you know that."

Yeah, he definitely knew that. He could feel himself starting to get worked up, the anger rumbling around inside of him. His mom didn't mean it this way, but it was really easy to take away that what was most important was his dad's job. It isn't fair that it didn't matter what Avery said or how scared he is, nothing was going to change.

Therefore, he chooses not to argue, and says, "Are you guys going to catch him?" He looks back and forth between his dad and Lt. Weatherby.

"We've put a call in to every hospital, urgent care, and veterinarian, basically anyone that you pay to clean and stitch up a wound," says Chief Fowler. "The surrounding departments have also been made aware. If we don't get him on the island, we will get him when he goes for medical attention. Don't worry. We'll get him."

Avery can't bring himself to remind his dad that he said the same thing about Officer Brown's killer, and there have been no answers to that.

A sharp sound cuts through the moment of quiet. It's only Chief Fowler's phone vibrating against the table, but Avery feels as though his heart stopped from the shock of it. He hopes no one notices his shallow breaths or hears his heart pounding through his chest.

His dad gets up from the table and starts walking towards the back door before he answers the phone. A work call, and he always wanders away when one of those comes in. In his absence, Mrs. Weatherby points out the time.

"Boys, you should maybe try to sleep. Would you rather sleep in the living room or Landon's room?" she asks.

"If it's okay, Mrs. Weatherby, could we stay out here in the living room?" asks Owen. "Thor is settled on his bed in here, and I think the three of us prefer to stay with the dogs."

Avery knows he does. Thor saved his life. Wow.

Thor. Saved. His. Life.

The parents get busy cleaning dishes off the table. Lt. Weatherby reminds Landon of where the extra pillows and sleeping bags are. He even offers to blow up a few mattresses. Everyone seems to have a task, but Avery just sits in his seat at the table, unable to move.

He jumps when his mom wraps her arms around him.

"Oh, bear, you're shaking. I'm so sorry this happened, that I wasn't there to protect you," his mom whispers in his ear.

"You can't be with me every second of the day, Mom," Avery whispers back.

For a minute, all the hustle in the room goes quiet, and his mom is the only thing he sees and hears.

"You're so strong, do you know that? You handled that situation exactly as you should have. I am so grateful that you are okay, and that you are my son," says Mrs. Fowler, holding Avery close to her.

Normally, this is when he would make a sarcastic comment or say something about how she's loving him to death. But not tonight. All he wants is for his mom to stay holding him close, keeping him safe.

"Is there room for me in this hug?" asks Chief Fowler. Avery didn't even hear his dad come back inside, but now he's here wrapping his arms around Avery's mom's.

"I just wish I could keep you safe inside of one of those little hamster balls or something," says Avery's mom.

"Oh, Emily. You want him to have friends, don't you?" Chief Fowler says, and Avery laughs because his dad is just such a kid sometimes. "Besides, I have good news. We found our guy."

"They're sure it's him?" asks Lt. Weatherby, calling from the kitchen.

"The wound on the arm matches the description, as does height and location," the chief says. "Emily, I figure you can come down to the station and identify him, and this way Avery doesn't have to be involved."

Avery pushes against his parents to get some air and see their faces. "Isn't it a little late for that?" he asks.

"I just thought you wouldn't want to have to confront him again," says his dad, "and that you'd rather not have to deal with it."

Rather not have to deal with it, Avery thinks. He's afraid to close his eyes tonight, so he has no choice but to be dealing with it.

"I would rather know for sure it was the right guy," says Avery, "and the only way to do that is to be there myself. When do we go?"

"Well, I'm going to head back to the station now, so I can come get you first thing in the morning," says the chief.

"You're going to sleep at the station?" Avery's mom asks.

The chief mumbles that there is a lot of work that needs to get done and needs to get done now, and Mrs. Fowler says in just as low of a voice that she just thought that after what happened… So at least this is normal, thinks Avery. His father will be at work. In a world where everything has turned upside down, this is the same.

***

The three boys lie sprawled out in the Weatherby's living room, Owen on the couch and Landon and Avery each on an inflatable mattress lined up in front of the couch. Avery's nestled between Thor and Hulk, their furry heads settled close to his. Cartoon Network is on the television, and though Avery isn't actually watching it, he finds the flashes of color and the snippets of sound bites comforting. It's like being a kid on a Saturday morning. Well, he is a kid, though it's hard to still feel like it.

"Do you want to talk about it, Avery?" asks Landon with some hesitation.

"There isn't much to say really. It happened so fast," says Avery. "I turned around, and he was there. I yelled for help and tried to open the window. Thor and Hulk protected me. My mom showed up just after the guy stabbed Thor. He said for me to tell my dad that he isn't wanted here, then my mom came in and he shoved her and ran. End of story."

"He said your dad wasn't wanted here?" asks Owen. He's sitting cross legged on the couch, a blanket wrapped around his head and shoulders. "I hate to point this out, but since you guys got here, all kinds of crazy things have happened, starting with what happened to Officer Brown."

"You think this is all connected? That whoever killed Officer Brown had something to do with the theft of her boots, the break-in at Ramsey's hardware store, and what happened to Avery?" asks Landon, still curled on his side, reaching out to pet Hulk.

"I know I am not the brains of the operation here, but it's possible," says Owen. "At least, I think it's possible. When you think about what Mr. Fountain said today, some people would have been unhappy that the Fowlers showed up. Officer Brown was already causing problems."

Landon sits up and turns to look at Owen. "And then they silence the problem, and make it look like Fowler can't handle it.

The SBI has to solve the case with no crime scene and no witnesses. Then evidence goes missing on his watch, and then an unsolvable break-in. Then a threat, or I guess an attack. I don't really know what to call tonight."

"Terrifying. That's what I call it," says Avery.

A few minutes go by without talking, just the sounds of dogs panting and recorded laughter, the fan whirring above.

"We give up. We're out of our league, and it's better for us to just leave it up to our dads," says Landon. "Let's just go back to our regularly scheduled summer break."

"But what about Officer Brown?" Owen asks.

The silence gets uncomfortable. It meant everything to Avery to catch Officer Brown's murderer, but he's afraid. Up until now, the danger felt completely separate from what they were doing. That feeling is gone.

"I don't know that I can do it, guys," says Avery.

"It's okay, Avery. We understand," says Landon.

But Avery didn't think it was, or that it would be.

Chapter 23

They were in the back of the sandwich shop, munching on the last of their chips. Avery appreciated the privacy this corner of the restaurant provided. Plenty of potted plants seemed to provide a shelter from everyone's eyes. He still had the police station on his mind. His dad asked the man to step forward, and even though Avery knew that the man couldn't see him, it was intimidating.

"Do you feel any better now?" asks Landon.

"Yes and no," says Avery. "I'm happy that the guy is locked up, but I can't help but wonder who he's working with. The fact that my dad's still at work, after having been there all night, says that he's really concerned."

Landon tries to respond, but his voice is gobbled up by the noise from another table. There was a group of older men a few tables over, and the plants couldn't protect the boys from having to hear their conversation. It was loud and boisterous, a moaning and groaning session.

Avery could hear a voice say, "Do they have any leads?"

That piqued his interest. Leads on what? Are these men talking about what happened to him last night? How do people know about that?

A voice answers, "Nothing. How hard can it actually be, you know? You fingerprint stuff, ask for witnesses. I mean, I know the security camera failed, but police officers have solved crimes for decades without that kind of technology. If Fowler can't do it, why do we have him here?"

Avery can't see any of these men's faces, but he feels confident the voice he just heard belongs to Mr. Ramsey.

"Is that who I think it is?" Avery asks, his eyes wide with disbelief. His cheeks are fully red, angry at how his father is being spoken about, and angrier that he can do absolutely nothing about it.

Owen shushes him and reclines back in his seat more; he is the closest to the table full of men.

"Well, you're one of the town managers, you have to know of a way to get rid of him," another voice says.

"Trust me, I'm working on it," says the voice Avery thinks is Ramsey. Then there is a round of laughter.

"Alright, we aren't paranoid. They're plotting to get rid of your dad, Avery," whispers Landon.

Avery feels as though steam must be coming out of his ears. His father is an incredible police officer. Whatever is going on here, it has nothing to do with his inability to do his job.

"Let's go, guys. I can't listen to these clowns anymore," says Owen. The boys get up from their table and walk past the table of men single file, each one glaring at the men there. They don't flinch when the men laugh harder.

The sunshine doesn't bring Avery any comfort or joy. He sees the tourists flowing past him, enjoying their ice cream or their smoothies, basking in this picture-perfect day. But it isn't perfect. It's all a lie.

He sees Landon step away and press his phone against his ear, but he's too consumed with his frustration to care.

"Man, they are making all of our dads look like jokes and then trash talking them out in public," says Owen. "They know how people listen and then go run their mouths. This is such garbage!"

Landon joins them back on the sidewalk, and they start walking, no particular destination set.

"I know we agreed last night that we shouldn't try to follow Mr. Ramsey or Dr. Amando. It's dangerous and reckless and stupid. For sure," says Landon. "But Carter just called me. Mr. Ramsey's plane is in the hanger. He said some randos just delivered it back to its usual spot. He also said that no one was going to be around for a while if we wanted to take a look."

"Not for nothing, that guy is a creep. But what do we think we're going to do?" asks Owen. "Call the cops if we find something, and they'll just turn a blind eye that we're trespassing on someone's aircraft? We already got away with that at Officer Brown's house. I don't think we'll be lucky twice."

"No, but if we do find something, we finally shut those guys up," says Avery. "I'm in, Landon. Owen, if you don't want to go, I understand." He looks at his friend with a small smile to show he means it.

"Really, when have I ever seemed like the one who would bail out on this?" asks Owen.

"Literally, just now," Avery says, rolling his eyes.

"When'd you get so gullible? Let's go," says Owen. "Just don't forget to text your dad, Avery, and tell him where we're going."

***

The hanger sits quietly in the island's center. It looks much like a cloud itself, all white aluminum paneling, a rounded roof, big enough to house an indoor soccer field with three huge bay doors, much like a garage.

Avery feels overcome with awe when he walks inside. The planes are sleek and shiny, well displayed under the endless rows of lights. The ceiling is exposed to create tremendous height and space inside the hanger, and it gives the illusion that the lights go on forever. But the planes, they are beautiful. It's enough to make Avery want to take flying lessons with Carter. His eyes are bright and wide, and he begins to reach a hand toward the closest plane, then recoils, realizing that he could get Carter in trouble.

Carter must notice because he tells Avery it's okay. "Did you guys want a tour?" Carter asks. "We have keys to all of the planes in case we need to move them around, and some owners pay us to clean and service the planes, so it's not a big deal if you wanted to look inside one or two of those."

"Sweet! Lemme in one of these guys!" shouts Owen. He clamors past Avery and Landon and runs to an apple red plane.

"Nice choice," Carter says. "This one is a Cirrus Vision SF50. It's actually a jet, and it's got an intense engine on it, so it flies with the smoothness of a cruise liner. Do you see how it's crafted differently than some of the others by having the horizontal stabilizers more vertical? We can all go up in there; it seats about five."

The smell of the leather seats, the feeling of that leather, smooth as butter, and the plush carpet under their feet, Avery can't believe this is how some people travel, and he hasn't even been in the cockpit yet. The amount of buttons and levers seems overwhelming, but Carter explains what each one does, why it's important.

"You're really good at this, Carter. I can totally see why you like spending time here," says Avery.

"You should come up in the air some time. Because this? This is nothing," Carter says.

They climb back down from the SF50 and wander over to one that is striped like a candy cane and looks like a helicopter and a plane had a baby. Carter tells them that it's a hydroplane. Its wings are retractable, and it can basically become a boat.

"That's bananas!" Avery says. "How do people afford these things?"

"Some aren't as expensive. You guys have just picked some of the more impressive ones off the bat. Here, look at this one," Carter says, leading them over to a yellow plane with a propeller on its nose. "Its fuselage is much smaller; it can only carry two people and has a very small cargo hold behind the seats. But the flight controls and panel look pretty similar."

Because it's a much smaller plane, the boys take turns exploring it, but despite how much simpler this plane is compared to the others, Avery's interest is greater because this plane is similar to the one owned by Mr. Ramsey. It's obviously not meant for family vacations; it's too small for that.

"Carter, why would someone get a plane like this instead of one like the first plane you showed us?" Avery asks.

"Well, size is obviously different; this one isn't meant for people as much as it is just a storage container," he begins, "but it's also kind of a toy. This is the kind of plane you'd expect to see doing the rolls and loops. It won't go as fast as that first plane or as far, either."

Avery nods his head, wondering what the magic words are to get them onto Mr. Ramsey's plane.

In the distance, he can hear a high-pitched ringing noise, pulsing almost like a phone. Carter says he needs to go deal with that.

"But you guys can look around. There's the plane you were asking about," Carter says before jogging away towards the sound of the ringing.

Owen is the first to reach Ramsey's plane, and when he pulls on the door to the fuselage, it's locked, denying him entry.

"Dude, did you really think if it had any kind of drugs in

there, he would just leave it unlocked for anyone to find?" Landon asks. He climbs up on the wings to try to see inside the plane. "Hey, there is definitely something in here, though. What did Officer Brown say that she saw those guys handing over?"

"Suitcases. Large suitcases," Avery says, now climbing up to see what Landon can see.

"Did she say what color because these are black?"

"Landon, come on, man, that proves nothing. About a bajillion people in the world probably have black luggage," says Owen.

Avery agrees with Owen; without getting a look inside those suitcases, they can't be sure anything suspect is happening here.

"What exactly are you doing climbing all over my plane?" asks a large, booming voice.

Avery feels like his blood has gone cold. He doesn't want to turn around to see who the voice came from. The shock of hearing it was enough. His pulse quickens, his heart pounds. Owen and Landon turn their heads just enough so that the three of them are looking at each other, each with eyes wide and deep frowns. Together, they turn around to see who is speaking to them.

None of the boys speak up. Mr. Ramsey stands below them, his cheeks flushed with red, and probably not from the heat outside. He yells again, telling them to speak for themselves and to get down immediately.

Slowly, carefully, the boys sit, letting their legs and feet dangle off the sides of the wings before they hop to the ground.

"Look, we didn't mean any disrespect. We were just looking at the planes," says Owen. "Avery over here has an interest in aviation and we just thought-"

A twisted smile appears on Mr. Ramsey's face; it isn't comforting to see. It makes Avery even more panicked. In a quick movement, Ramsey reaches out and grabs Owen by the front of his shirt. Owen drops his chin and raises his arms as if in surrender.

"You obviously were not thinking about much. Why is it that you are always sneaking around somewhere, huh?" Ramsey asks.

"We were actually invited here," Owen tries again.

"You should stop speaking. I am far more interested in what your buddies have to say," Ramsey says. He still grips Owen's shirt.

"Copy that," says Owen.

"Well, Landon, you had so much to say the last time we ran into each other, what's happened? Cat got your tongue?" asks Ramsey. "What are your fathers going to say about this?"

Avery sees some movement coming from the far corner of the hanger. He first thinks it's Carter coming back, but he realizes this person is too tall and too old. He squints to try to get a better visual, holding his breath until he can make out a face.

It's Mr. Fitzgerald, Officer Brown's neighbor. What's he doing here?

But Mr. Fitzgerald walks briskly to where the boys are with Mr. Ramsey, his arms pumping fiercely in time with his feet. His face is drawn, mouth in a line.

"Put the boy down! What's wrong with you?" asks Mr. Fitzgerald, knocking Ramsey's hand away from Owen and stepping in between Owen and Ramsey.

The three friends take a step back slowly, silently, but Ramsey turns and sees them.

"You're not going anywhere!" he shouts, attempting to take a step towards them.

Again, Mr. Fitzgerald puts his body between Ramsey and the boys, throwing his arms up in defense.

"Let them out of here, they did nothing. They are children, and not just any children, but children of police officers," Mr. Fitzgerald says.

"I don't know that they did nothing! They were climbing all over my plane," Ramsey says to him, his voice lower now. "You keep an eye on them while I climb up and make sure nothing has been tampered with."

Ramsey brushes past Mr. Fitzgerald, staring down the boys as he begins to climb up to the fuselage and enter the plane. Avery can hear him rattling around inside it.

"Boys, why did you have to stay involved?" Mr. Fitzgerald asks, shaking his head and staring up at the plane.

"We told you, sir. She was our friend," says Landon softly.

"She was somebody that put her nose into other people's business one too many times. Much like you boys have done. And you see where that got her," Ramsey says, resurfacing from the inside of the plane.

"Well, now that you've seen that no one messed with your stuff, we're going to go now," says Avery. He takes a step away from the plane, and Owen and Landon begin to follow him.

"I've already told you, you're not going anywhere until you tell me what you were doing," Ramsey says loudly, belligerently. He hoists himself down to the ground and puts his finger in Avery's face. "You're not calling the shots here!"

Avery's legs shake below him in response to Ramsey's aggression and anger. He is close enough that Avery feels Ramsey's hot breath on his face. Avery tries to step back, but Ramsey snatches the back of his neck and squeezes, turning him around to face his friends.

"Let me go; you're hurting me, and you can't keep us here! You have no right!" Avery shouts. He tries to swing his arms, to shift his weight to break loose, but Ramsey's grip won't relent.

"It's about time you learn how this island works, kid" Ramsey says through gritted teeth. "For the last time, what were you doing on my plane?"

Again, Mr. Fitzgerald intervenes, swatting at Ramsey's arms. It's then that Avery notices the angry red marks racing on his skin, cuts and scratches on Mr. Fitzgerald's right arm. Cuts that could have been made when breaking into Officer Brown's house, unless Mr. Fitzgerald is in possession of a really gnarly cat.

Now Avery is even more confused and more on alert. He first felt relief that there was an adult to help them, but maybe he shouldn't. Mr. Fitzgerald seems so kind. Why would he have wanted to hurt Officer Brown?

"We saw a picture of your plane, and I wanted to see it for myself," says Avery with as much strength as he can muster. His voice wobbles slightly, and his brain races to find the words to say next.

Ramsey and Mr. Fitzgerald both still as Avery's words hit them. Ramsey squints and focuses his eyes directly on Avery's, pulling him close.

"Saw a picture where?" Ramsey asks. His voice is measured and low, his breath fast. His cheeks are flooded with red.

"You know where," says Avery, barely above a whisper.

Ramsey shoves Avery backwards, sending him sprawling to the ground. Ramsey pulls out his phone, but as he lifts his phone to his ear a thunderous BOOM in the front of the hanger steals all of their attention. Twenty officers from various departments rush in like a flood of water, weapons drawn, and they're shouting at the two men to put their hands up.

Mr. Fitzgerald immediately does as he's told. He stands silently and waits for an officer to come and place him in handcuffs. He does not argue or resist, though he does wince when the cold metal hits the scratches on his arm.

Two officers come alongside the boys. One helps Avery up off the ground while the other asks if they are hurt.

"No, I think we're okay," says Landon. "You guys made it here just in time."

The officers ask for the boys to come with them, but Avery at least is not ready to peel his eyes off the scene in front of him.

Ramsey is shouting and cursing at the officers attempting to secure him. One deputy stands in front of him, guarding the boys, and another is grabbing one of Ramsey's arms and jerking it behind his back in order to get the handcuffs on.

Finally, Chief Fowler strolls over to the commotion. He nods in Avery's direction, but other than that, keeps his focus on Ramsey. His lips are slightly up turned, and his voice is calm.

"Mitchell Ramsey, you are under arrest for the unlawful detainment of minors, crimes against justice via fake police report, obstruction of justice, tampering with evidence, and conspiracy to commit murder. The narcotics charges, I'm sure, will be added later. You have the right to remain silent," says Chief Fowler.

"What do you think you are going to pull off here, Fowler? You come in here thinking you know how to handle these situations, but this here is a small town. You shouldn't go looking for trouble when there isn't any. You just make things worse for yourself and all around you," Mr. Ramsey protests, trying to keep his arms free, unwilling to be restrained. Two officers came to assist the first, grabbing hold of Ramsey roughly to make their point.

"Is that you trying to threaten my family?" Chief Fowler asks, his eyes narrowed in and voice brimming with anger.

"That's me telling you that we run this island, not you."

"Well, I don't know how much running of anything you will be doing from a prison cell," Fowler returns confidently.

Chapter 24

Family dinner tonight looks a little different, but it is still family dinner. Because the chief can't leave just yet, there is too much to do, Mrs. Fowler brought a picnic to the police station, and Avery sits with his parents around his father's desk, the painting his mother created of Avery in the surf above their heads, the buzz of the police station around them. His friends sit with their families similarly at different desks. The chairs aren't all that comfortable, the silverware is plastic, but it is still such a good feeling, sitting with his family, thinks Avery.

"How did you know we were in trouble, Dad?" Avery asks.

His father, who loves macaroni and cheese and would much rather sit in silence and enjoy the food in front of him, sighs deeply before answering.

"I knew because of Mr. Fitzgerald," says the chief. "He agreed to work with us to provide evidence in our case against Mr. Ramsey." He takes a bite of his macaroni and cheese and smiles like a small child.

"But why would he do that?" asked Avery. "He's the one that broke into Officer Brown's house."

The chief looks up from his food, his eyebrows scrunched together. He puts his fork down. "What makes you think that Fitzgerald had anything to do with the break-in?"

"The scratches on his arm," says Avery. "He had tried to cover them with long sleeves the other day, but seeing as they don't have a pet and he was right by the crime scene, it seemed like a logical assumption."

Chief Fowler chuckles a little before putting another bite into his mouth.

"Well, am I right?" Avery asks.

"Those are some fine detective skills you're honing. And it's the reason he agreed to work with us. Forensics found evidence connecting him to the burglary and he agreed to flip," says the chief.

"So did Mr. Ramsey have Officer Brown killed?" Avery asks, the excitement in his voice now gone.

"I'm not a judge, Avery," the chief answers, his tone matched to Avery's.

"But you arrested him for conspiracy to commit murder, so that's what you think, right?" Avery asks again.

Chief Fowler exhales deeply, and Mrs. Fowler sits back in her seat. She had asked earlier in the night if they could avoid police talk, but Avery has a different agenda.

"Yes, considering all the evidence, that is what I think," his dad says.

"Regardless, you have enough to make the SBI reconsider their stance on how Officer Brown died, right?" asks Mrs. Fowler. Avery smiles at his mom, happy that they are united in wanting the town to know Officer Brown did not do this to herself.

"Actually, the SBI was already reconsidering their statement," the chief says. "They granted me authorization to have a psychological autopsy done on Officer Brown. This is when a trained mental health professional does their best to create an in-depth reconstruction of an unclear death. This doctor, a third-party, no ties to the island whatsoever, spoke with every last person he thought might be helpful to this case. And he feels that there are plenty of factors that show she would not have done this to herself. Like, past stressful instances that she handled with ease and the fact that she seemed hopeful for the future, not just because there was a new chief in town, but because she had applied to other agencies. She had a plan for the future. Her behavior the day in question was completely normal. Basically, he says that the report originally given to the SBI was completely wrong. To use it in court, we'll need to get a second opinion, but it was enough to convince the SBI to let me keep looking."

"But what made you go after Mr. Ramsey?" asks Avery.

"You did, actually," says the chief. "When Andrew sent me the footage, it offered more than what Mr. Ramsey's footage did, which tipped the SBI off to foul play. However, with the doctor's report on her mental state and the lack of a crime scene…but the video footage was what linked it all because the owner of the mystery car is the same man that tried to attack you. And he and the Callaway kid, the one who stole the boots, weren't too good with keeping secrets. And thanks to a resident's Ring camera, we learned that Ramsey broke into his own store."

"Wow, I can't believe you were able to do all of that, Dad," says Avery.

"I won't lie, you and your friends did help us wrap up the Callaway issue fast, but the other things we just needed to follow the clues and rely on technology," says the chief. "Ramsey, Fitzgerald, and Callaway, they aren't well practiced criminals. The last chief was willing to tolerate the drugs moving through the island, so they have never had to work to cover things up."

Avery considers this and how it makes sense with everything that Officer Brown had written about in her journals. The police chief would not allow her to make any waves because he was allowing for the drugs, and the money that goes along with them, to cycle through the island.

"Well it's more than just Ramsey, right?" asks Avery. "What comes next in ending this?"

He sees his parents exchange a look. Avery can tell they've discussed this; it's their we're on the same page look. And it's annoying.

"Avery, you have a great eye for detail, and you're very brave and analytical," his dad says. "I'm so proud of you for how you have handled everything this summer, starting with the move, you have made new friends, you fought for what's right, you've fought for yourself, and you've learned so much about guitar, surfing, and who you want to be. But you don't need to know what comes next because you're thirteen, and I want you to be thirteen and safe."

"But Dad, we were able to-" Avery begins.

"Avery, you don't seem to understand how much danger you have been in, how much danger you have put yourself in recently," says Mrs. Fowler. "Yes, you might make a great detective someday, but that day is not today. Today you got lucky. I don't want to know how long that luck lasts. Your detective days are over for right now."

Avery slumps in his chair, forgetting about the dinner in front of him completely. He thinks about all of the clues he, Landon, and Owen found, the dead ends they hit, but how something else kept revealing itself, with time and patience. He could be patient, he could do this. Why won't his parents see how capable he is, even if he is only thirteen?

"Oh, and Avery, don't think that I don't know you guys were all up in Officer Brown's house," says Chief Fowler, turning his head to the side in disbelief. "Your prints are all over the place. Your mom and I think being attacked and almost abducted is enough of a punishment, but I don't want to have this conversation again."

"Yes, sir."

"Now finish your dinner. You know how I feel about wasting food," the chief says.

Chapter 25

Avery ties the laces on his cleats and takes a swig of water before running out onto the field. Coach Gilmore starts clinics each morning with a run, and even though it is early, it is hot, the sun brutal and unforgiving and the breeze from the ocean not making it to the fields.

It may be hot, but clinics are helpful. Meeting the other guys on the team and getting back into running has been a nice change for Avery. By the end of each morning, exhaustion courses through Avery's veins, though somehow, he still finds a way to get to guitar lessons with Andrew and go surfing with Landon and Owen. This is the new normal. Everything has been such a blur since moving to Summerset Island, the town he thought would be sleepy and boring. He will never think that again.

It has only been a few weeks since someone broke into his house and then tried to abduct him and his friends. The story spread through the island like wildfire, though, so he came into soccer practice like something of a living legend. He and his family are back in their house, his bedroom no longer a crime scene. His mother and father worked tirelessly to assemble the new furniture and rearranged it a number of times before finally agreeing to its placement. Chief Fowler has declared that HGTV is no longer allowed in the house. Mrs. Fowler still asks when she is getting her vacation.

Avery brings his mind back to the clinic, to the one against two dribble drill he is currently facing. Coach Gilmore paces the field, taking notes on every player. Avery feels confident in his actions, especially when he manages to keep the ball in his possession. Practice ends, and Landon shouts to Avery that they will meet him at the beach after lunch as they hop onto their bikes. Avery knows his mom will be happy to only have to feed him. He pedals quickly, despite being tired from practice. At home, Thor and Hulk greet him at the door like usual. Thor's wound is healing nicely, and he finally is allowed to keep the cone off his head, which is good because he kept trying to attack it.

Mrs. Fowler is just putting the finishing touches on their sandwiches. Even though he is sweaty and gross, she pulls him in for a hug. Avery details all that happened at soccer today.

"I really want to do well this year, especially if Dad will be at the games," admits Avery.

"Bear, he will be proud of you as long as you do your best, whatever that means. Just compare yourself to yesterday, not to anyone else on the field, okay?" He agrees, and then remembers to tell her that his friend Matt said hello.

"I'm glad you're still checking in with him. What does he think of your summer?" Mrs. Fowler asks before chomping on a carrot stick.

"He wants to know when he can come visit."

His mom laughs and rolls her eyes, but she suggests he come before school starts, and Avery rushes to call him immediately.

***

That night, the Weatherby and the Martinez families come to the Fowler home for a barbeque. They sit outside and appreciate the colors of the sky and the generous breeze coming off the dunes. There's music playing and frisbees flying around, the smell of hamburgers makes people's mouths water. It's a celebration. This week, two other town managers were arrested for participating in drug trafficking. As Chief Fowler has been saying since the beginning, in small towns people like to talk.

There is still a lot of work to do. The court date is weeks away, but the families are celebrating because the State Bureau of Investigation announced that the case was a murder, and now they will be assisting the state with the trial against Mr. Ramsey. Avery had almost been attacked, he had almost been abducted, but he is fine, and he is watching justice be served and enjoying the remaining summer with his friends and family.

The parents are relaxing around the firepit; the moon is high in the sky, it's the perfect night to play soccer on the beach. However, Landon, Owen, and Avery have sprawled out in Avery's room. Avery is on the floor, the dogs sandwiching him as usual. Landon collapses on the couch and props his head up on the arm rest, and Owen is on the bed and reaching for the Magic 8-Ball.

"Did we ever decide if this thing really works?" Owen asks.

"I mean, if we look at it from a scientific standpoint, it did, right? We asked those questions and every one of them was right," offers Landon.

Avery stays quiet, but he likes to think that the Magic 8-Ball has been helping him all along. He has had adventures, no question of that.

"Will I be team captain this year?" Owen asks and turns the ball over. He scowls at the response. Don't count on it. Landon and Avery howl in laughter, and it feels good.

"Alright, wise guy, has Avery seen the last of Marissa?" asks Owen.

Definitely not and another roar of laughter.

Owen tosses the ball to Avery.

"Ugh, enough with your cheese fest," says Avery over the laughter of the other two. "How about, will we solve another mystery together?"

That gets the other boys' attention. He turns the ball over to read signs point to yes.

"Maybe we just focus on school and soccer and not getting ourselves killed first before we take on anything else?" says Landon.

"Maybe, but we had fun, right?" Owen asks.

They had fun, and Avery's dad was right. He learned a lot about people, about justice, and about himself. He wants to think he's not done helping people find their truths.

Who knows what this soccer season will bring, or what the

year has in store for them? For tonight, they are safe and happy, and all seems right in their home on Summerset Island.

Acknowledgements

Much like raising a child, there are a village of people to thank for helping me make this book a reality. In no particular order, here it goes...

To my Avery, for helping me "research" by watching the Hardy Boys on Hulu with me. And thank you for putting up with the many, many mornings I sat during breakfast typing away, the movie nights that I disrupted your viewing to get out an idea. I promise to always support you in at least the same way.

To my parents for encouraging me to be a reader, especially my mom who had no shortage of Agatha Christie or Mary Higgins Clark on hand. Thank you for the hours and hours spent watching Murder She Wrote and Columbo together when I was a kid.

To Miki for always encouraging me and for your willingness to always be a beta reader, even in early stages. I am pretty sure your bias skews a great deal of things, but I love you for it anyway.

To Amy Spalding for being an amazing book coach, for your thoughtful feedback and provoking suggestions.

To Gabe Lovejoy for telling me that I was ridiculous to think that only three people would read my book and for the amazing cover art.

To Beth and Julie who listened to me ramble on and on about whether or not the writing is any good, who to publish with, and if self-publishing is just like a runner's up trophy. Thanks for always being active participants in my crazy brain and for bringing a fresh perspective when I need it.

To Brittany, Heather, Krysten, and Stephanne for supporting this project in one way or another and helping me to realize that it can be done if I'm willing to work for it.

To my local Port City Java baristas for the iced coffee and workspace, for the quiet that wasn't really quiet at all but was just what I needed.

To the many other people who inspired or encouraged me in one way or another, I am grateful to you as well, and to each person who picks up this book to read it. Thank you just doesn't seem to be enough, but it's all I've got.

About the Author

photo credit Jack Upton

Melissa Puritis fell in love with reading as soon as she could hold a book in her hands and with mysteries thanks to Nancy Drew. Now, she gets to share her love of stories and words with her middle school students. When she's not in the classroom, Melissa can be found with her son, Avery, exploring the mountains or lounging on the beaches of North Carolina. Completed with the help of a Taylor Swift soundtrack and a diet of iced coffee and Twizzlers, Shadows by the Lighthouse is her first novel.

Made in the USA
Columbia, SC
02 January 2022